Srilaaji

Srilaaji

THE GILDED LIFE AND LONGINGS OF A MARWARI GOODWIFE

SHOBHAA DÉ

SIMON & SCHUSTER

London · New York · Sydney · Toronto · New Delhi

A CBS COMPANY

First published in India by Simon & Schuster India, 2020
A CBS company

1 3 5 7 9 10 8 6 4 2

Simon & Schuster India
818, Indraprakash Building,
21, Barakhamba Road,
New Delhi 110001

www.simonandschuster.co.in

PB ISBN: 978-93-86797-83-4
eBook ISBN: 978-93-86797-84-1

This is a work of fiction. Names, characters, organisations, places, events and incidents are either products of the author's imagination or used fictitiously.

Typeset in India by SÜRYA, New Delhi

Printed and bound in India by Replika Press Pvt. Ltd.

Simon & Schuster India is committed to sourcing paper that is made from wood grown in sustainable forests and support the Forest Stewardship Council, the leading international forest certification organisation. Our books displaying the FSC logo are printed on FSC certified paper.

Na jao saiyaan chhuda ke baiyan
Kasam tumhari main ro padoongi

Shakeel Badayuni
Sahib Bibi Aur Ghulam (1962)

To the never-say-die spirit of Srilaaji ...
and to our uncrushable courage as women.

PART ONE

Srilaaji's Fantasy

I am twelve years old and lying naked on my large four poster bed, with three pillows between my thighs. I am making love to the pillows. But in a gentle, unhurried way. There is an enormous painting of an English Duke on the wall opposite my bed. He is astride a horse with an enormous erection. The Duke is staring fixedly at me—as if encouraging me to go ahead and reach an orgasm. I keep trying, adjusting the pillows, altering my position—nothing works! I almost get there—and phut! It's back to base. The Duke laughs derisively, gets off his horse and walks to the bed, his blue eyes shining, his white teeth gleaming. His rider's crop whistles as he cracks it across my bare buttocks. I squeeze the pillows harder and harder ... still nothing happens. The Duke lifts me up and throws me onto the saddle. The horse snorts and gets up on his hind legs. The Duke looks at me quizzically, but I shake my head vehemently and say, 'Nooooooo!' The Duke dismounts and starts caressing the horse ... I watch them intently. I no longer need to squeeze the pillows.

VIRGIN

I touched my thighs and they were sticky. I wanted to rush to the bathroom immediately, but that would not have been possible just then. It was Bijoya Dashmi, and the married ladies had just finished playing 'sindoor khela' in our Bengali neighbour's marble courtyard with other married ladies from the family, and a few friends. I had wanted to join the ladies, but Buaji said sternly, 'You are a virgin … you cannot play this game.'

I didn't know the meaning of 'virgin'—I was eleven years old.

'What is a virgin?' I asked Buaji, staring at her many beautiful bangles and rings, as she reached for a heavy silver thali and deftly arranged the mithai.

'All of this is made in our kitchen …' she mentioned with pride. 'No bazaar mithai in this house … at least, so long as I am alive.'

At other times, the aroma of fresh ghee would have drawn me to the ladoos, especially to the besan ones with kishmish. But today, I was waiting for her to answer my question.

I noticed she was avoiding looking directly at me. So I repeated, 'Buaji ... what is a virgin? How do you know I am a virgin? I want to play with all the maasis and have sindoor on my face.' Buaji held my chin and brought her own face very close to mine. 'A virgin is a pure girl ... untouched. Intact. Poori-poori. You understand? You stop being a virgin only after you get married. Those ladies are married. They are not virgins. Only married ladies can cover each other with sindoor. If you do that, Ma Durga will get very angry and punish you.'

The stickiness between my thighs had turned into a trickle. I wasn't sure whether I had urinated by mistake. My eyes searched the large room. I was looking for my mother. As usual, she was not there.

Calling out to Chumkididi was not an option. She was the elderly maid servant who looked after me and her presence inside the family function at that moment was not required. I was now of the age when the elders felt I could look after myself in adult company without a maid standing by in attendance. Well, they were wrong. I needed Chumkididi all the time. She slept in my room at night. And even in the afternoons during my summer holidays. I wanted her to take me to the bathroom right now. How could I get up? There would be a wet patch on my clothes—the new ones I had been given a few hours ago. My mother would be most upset if a brand new set of clothes was ruined. I stayed put without moving. I refused to drink water or sip fruit juice, too afraid that more urine would come pouring out of my body without my having the slightest control over it. Oh God! What if the carpet and white gaddi I was seated on, also got damp?

Then, everybody would know something was wrong.

Buaji had moved away from me to look after the guests, some of whom had finished playing at our neighbour's and came over for nashta. The Bengali ones. In our home, we were very conscious of who was a Bengali-speaking Marwari, and who, the Bengali-speaking Bengali. Buaji would often say, 'Our women are different. They know how to behave themselves with men. But not those Bengali women—see how they are in the company of their husband's friends! Shamelessly flirting, making eyes, dropping their pallus, rolling their tongues inside their mouths in that way which men understand.'

Buaji had been monitoring the sindoor khela very closely for signs of bad behavior. This year there were more women than usual. Most were dressed in traditional, red-bordered white cotton sarees. They were dancing to a modernised version of Rabindra Sangeet and applying sindoor to each other's faces, making sure to fill the parting in the hair with a fistful of the vermilion. I was attracted to the colour. The women seemed to be having so much fun. But Buaji had said this game was not for me. Because I was a virgin. Without knowing I was a virgin.

I spotted Chumkididi carrying a large silver tray with silver bowls filled with badam-pistas. I called out to her, but she didn't hear because of the loud music. On any other day but this one, I would have got up and run towards her. But I dared not get up. My cousin Urmila came and sat down next to me. I shifted on the white gaddi to make place for her. And that's when I saw the stains, and let out a small cry. Nobody heard my cry, either. The music was deafening, and I could hear conch shells being blown to honour Ma Durga, and bid her a fitting goodbye as she made her way back to her celestial marital home in Mount Kailash, after briefly visiting her maternal family members on earth. I nudged Urmila urgently and pointed to the stain. Urmila was fourteen years old. She screamed, which startled me.

I asked, 'Am I going to die?'

And she laughed. I felt small and hurt, but Urmila continued to laugh. She ran off looking for Buaji, leaving me to sit miserably by myself, head lowered, and tears streaming down my flushed cheeks. When I looked up, I saw Chumkididi rushing towards me with a worried face. Right behind her was Buaji, who was quietly but firmly asking someone to summon my mother from wherever she was. So my fears were accurate—I *was* dying. Or else, why would my mother come to see me?

Buaji asked Chumkididi to go to her bedroom upstairs and bring down a few towels and a couple of bedsheets. Buaji kept her voice low and issued instructions in a near whisper, saying she didn't want anybody to notice what had happened. I was confused. My stomach had started to cramp. I had doubled up in pain and was feeling miserable. I was sure I was going to faint. Before dying. Maybe Buaji didn't want me to die in front of everybody and spoil the festival. She told me not to move till Chumkididi returned.

I started whimpering and asking for Ma. Buaji said shortly, 'She must be busy.'

I howled, 'I am dying ... I know I am dying ... I need Ma.'

Buaji placed a finger on her lips and said, 'You are not dying Srilaa. You have become a woman.' What? How was that even possible? I was just eleven years old.

~

The room was cool and fragrant. I was on Buaji's soft double mattress, under an even softer razai. I loved being in Buaji's huge room, with a silver mandir in one corner, and beautiful, heavy curtains which were rarely drawn. Buaji's room was permanently dark, and lit by her ornate bedside lamp. There was a deep red Kashmiri carpet on the polished marble floor. And heavy, teak wood almirahs lined the ivory-coloured walls. The almirahs were always locked. Buaji kept a bunch of keys tucked into her saree petticoat. She slept with them anchored there as well.

I was not alone in the room. Chumkididi was sitting

on the carpet, watching over me. I asked her what had happened to me, but she did not explain. I felt weak and was conscious of a thickish stuffing between my legs. I touched it suspiciously and withdrew my hand like I had received an electric shock.

'What is that thing?' I asked Chumkididi, who replied, 'It is to keep you clean, since from now on you will be unclean for five days of the month.'

Unclean? 'Where is Ma?' Chumkididi sighed and shrugged, 'She will be here soon ... try to sleep. You need rest.'

'Am I sick?' I asked worriedly.

'Not exactly ... but from now on, you will have to be more careful ... about everything. It's Ma Durga's boon that this happened to you on such a good day. Other girls are not so lucky.' Nothing was making any sense. I was lucky to be unclean and sick? 'Madamji will explain everything,' Chumkididi said, turning her face away.

My mother was called 'Madamji' by the staff. Only my mother. All the other ladies of her generation in our family were addressed as 'Bhabhiji'. Then there was Buaji. Who was called Buaji by all.

My legs felt like jelly. One side of my head was throbbing. And I had started to sweat, even though Buaji's room was cool (it never saw sunlight). Chumkididi was humming to herself and patting my feet absently, like she used to when I was a toddler, sleeping on her wide, comfortable lap.

'What is that thing between my legs?' I asked.

'It is something women use every month when they bleed. You will get used to it. I will show you how to clean yourself and how to wear that thing. Make sure nobody sees it. Change it four or five times a day. Hide it carefully from the male servants. Don't let anybody find it in the bathroom. And if you find blood stains on your knickers, rinse immediately. Don't worry, I will teach you how to protect yourself. Especially from men. What more can I tell you? It is every woman's curse. Now you are a woman, too. You will have to live with this monthly curse. Didn't Madamji explain all this to you?'

I was bleeding, Chumkididi had said. But I was not injured. Where was the blood coming from then? Why? Maybe Ma was delayed because she had gone to fetch our family doctor who would stop the bleeding. Maybe I was suffering from something fatal. Maybe I was dying.

As soon as I saw Chumkididi springing to her feet and straightening up, I knew Ma had entered the first door that led to Buaji's dressing area. I was right. Ma walked in briskly and looked at me in silence. She turned to Chumkididi and instructed her to bring tea. For some reason, I was feeling guilty. As if I had let Ma down in some way. She placed her delicate and beautiful hand with those tapering fingers over mine, and squeezed it.

'Darling!' she exclaimed cheerfully. 'Welcome to the club!' I laughed nervously, not sure which club she was welcoming me to. She checked her image in the large mirror over Buaji's dressing table and sighed, 'Thank God, I missed all the drama. And that horrible sindoor khela. Next they'll expect me to participate in the dhunuchi performance and dance with those paunchy men in dhotis.' She still hadn't told me which club I now belonged to.

It was okay. So long as she and I were together in the same club. She raised my razai and stared at my legs for a long time, as if she was searching for some clues. Then she said, 'I suppose I have to explain periods and all that boring stuff to you, now that you have started menstruating. Gosh! Rather too early, don't you think?'

I asked nervously, 'When is the doctor coming to make me stop bleeding?'

Ma laughed, 'You silly girl ... you really don't know a thing, do you? Oh dear ... okay, let's start with where the blood comes from ...' And that was my first and only conversation on the subject with Ma. Whatever else I needed to discover about monthly periods was done through mixed up conversations with Chumkididi. And later, with my class teacher, who informed me I was the first girl in my batch to get my 'chums'. She made it sound like it was all my fault.

Perhaps I was a freak? Would I be treated differently by the other girls once they found out? Would they stop playing with me? How come they were normal while I had become a 'woman' overnight? An eleven-year-old woman, whose tiny breasts had started to grow? Whose nipples had darkened, hardened and were sore to the touch? Whose hips had begun to widen? I was no longer me. I wanted to go back to that older me. I hated my new body. I hated bleeding every month. I hated the tension before my periods started. I hated wearing bulky sanitary pads. I hated waking up frequently at night to check whether I had stained the bedsheet with that peculiar coloured blood that oozed and oozed.

When I looked at myself in the bathroom mirror, I didn't like the pubic patch that had started to get thicker and thicker. I wanted to get rid of it somehow. But when I asked Chumkididi, she hid her face in her saree pallu and said, 'Chhhheee! What sort of questions you ask.'

I tried asking Ma once, but she had her manicurist over and was upset with the nail colour which she kept repeating was not 'pearly enough'. She had looked up distractedly to say, 'Oh, that! Darling you are too young for a Brazilian.' What had Brazil got to do with my pubic hair? Anyway, since the breasts were also growing, I would soon need bras. I loved the lace ones Ma always wore. I liked prying into her lingerie drawer.

Sometimes I would stumble upon crumpled notes, dried flowers, but my fascination was towards her pretty bras, especially the black ones. Ma looked her best before she got fully dressed. She would let me watch her as she lavished body oils, lotions and fragrances all over.

I once asked her, 'Why do you spray your armpits? Do people ask you to raise your arms and smell you there?'

Ma had replied breezily, 'Darling, you ask very awkward questions. When you get older I will explain feminine rituals to you.' And off she'd gone, a blur of French chiffon, a trail of French perfume ... her hair coiffed to perfection, Basra pearls at her throat, diamond clips on her earlobes, her favourite Patek Phillipe watch on her wrist ... and the multiple rings she frequently changed, gleaming on her slim fingers. But clad in her black bra and black lace panties, her feet shod in silk bedroom slippers, Ma resembled a painting, her face fresh and minus make-up, her skin radiant, her eyes dreamy. Ma was always lost in her own world. I had no access to her mysterious life outside our family home. I accepted Ma just as she was—aloof, disdainful, beautiful. And absent. Mainly, absent.

Buaji was different. She used to tell me it's okay if Ma was not around, so long as I had her and the others. 'Your Ma has her own life ...' she would say shortly, and change the subject. 'Ask me if you need anything. Chumki is always there to take care of you.'

I didn't want Buaji or Chumkididi, I wanted my Ma. I worshipped her! Oh yes, I also liked my father, the little I saw of him. He was called Babuji by everybody, and he was always busy. Ma and Babuji slept on different floors. My room was next to Buaji's, on the same floor as Ma's. All of us ate together on Babuji's floor which was below ours. This was because Babuji liked to be closer to the ground floor and next to the large kitchen. Why closer to the ground floor? That's where his personal staff stayed. He could keep an eye on the durwan and the main gate far better from his bedroom window, and he liked to wake up to the sounds of his seven cars being washed by the cleaners.

I hardly met Babuji, but whenever I did run into him, he would pat my head affectionately and say, 'Do your studies properly ... listen to your Buaji.' Sometimes he would look surprised and exclaim, 'Oh ... you have grown taller!' as if he had expected me to stay no higher than his knees my entire life. Those days, when I was four or five, Babuji would lift me up, laugh and say, 'You are my laadli ... my rajkumari ...' I would be overjoyed and rush to tell Chumkididi I had met my father.

I really wasn't sure if I wanted to become a 'woman'. I was not ready for it. Nothing about 'becoming a woman' sounded attractive to me. Become a woman—for what? The women around me were okay-okay. Not happy, not sad. I was not even a proper teenager yet, and I was already being told I had to become a woman. Made no sense. Just because I was bleeding. What difference did it make? I tried asking Buaji. She explained it was a very big thing. How?

'From now on, the world will see you differently, treat you differently. You will have to be extra cautious. Stay away from men.' Chumkididi had also said the same thing.

What did Buaji mean by asking me to stay away from

men? 'All men? Even Babuji and my favourite Prateek bhaiya?'

Buaji paused and answered carefully, 'No, not Babuji ... but the others ... especially drivers, gardeners and servants. Prateek bhaiya is a part of our family. He is okay. But make sure to take Chumki with you if you go to his home. Now that you are a big girl, you should stay away from strange men generally.'

I stared at her and she knew I was puzzled by her talk about staying away from men. She changed the subject and asked me how much I had scored in Math—my favourite subject.

'It is a good thing you understand numbers. Babuji could do with some help later. Had he had a son, things would have been different. But your Ma ...'

Buaji trailed off. Chumki told me later Ma had had a very difficult pregnancy when she was carrying me. She had nearly died. After my birth, she was weak and bedridden for months. Ma could not breastfeed me, and Buaji had hired two wet nurses when she realised Ma was not producing sufficient milk. Babuji had felt disappointed I was not a son, and made his displeasure known to Ma. Ma had started to believe it was all her fault for not producing a male child. Advised by the family doctor not to undergo another pregnancy, Ma decided to stay in the room where she had given birth to me. Buaji had said firmly, 'In our family, bahus do not give birth in hospitals in front of preying eyes.'

That's how the separate floors, separate rooms arrangement had started. And that's how it stayed.

I rarely visited my father in his room. It was not encouraged by Buaji. 'Babuji is a very busy man. No need to distract him,' she'd say, when I was ready to run straight in and show him my report card.

'I will tell him how well his laadli is doing in school ... now, go wash your hands.' I was constantly washing my hands as a young girl. Every adult member of our household would instruct me to wash my hands the minute they spotted me. My hands were not that dirty! At least not all the time.

Buaji was obsessed with cleanliness. She used her time in the long afternoons once lunch was done, to open one or two cupboards and sort out the contents, dusting even when there was no dirt. Chumkididi was her eager and able assistant, even if she complained of a backache after each clean up. Buaji would go looking for dirt all over the house. But she left Ma's chambers alone. I used to ask her why she didn't clean Ma's rooms. She'd say vaguely, 'Our timings don't match.' I wondered about Ma's timings. I asked Buaji where Ma went every day. She told me, 'Your mother does social work.' Buaji did not specify what sort of work.

When I asked Chumkididi, she said Ma worked in a very crowded area of Kolkata—what is called a bustee. She helped widows earn a living by stitching clothes, embroidering tablecloths and crocheting pretty doilies.

I was very impressed when I heard that. I asked Ma whether I could come with her when she visited poor people in bustees.

She looked surprised, arched her right eyebrow and laughed her tinkling laugh. 'Who told you I go to bustees to meet poor people?'

'You don't? Then where do you go?' Ma thought for a bit and said, 'I go to the Blind School to teach sightless people how to read and write.' I tried to visualise Ma helping blind children to read and write. I had eyes. I could see. But she never taught me how to read and write—it would have been so much easier. I kept quiet and told her solemnly I would come one day to meet her blind pupils. She smiled her sweet smile and kissed my forehead. I refused to let Chumkididi remove the trace of lipstick her mouth had left near my hairline.

~

A distant aunt from Kanpur was staying with us for a few days. Nobody liked this nosy woman who asked the price of everything. I saw her staring at me during dinner. She was staring pointedly at my chest. I had budding breasts but I was not old enough to wear a bra. Her looking at me that way, made me self-conscious and I kept my arms crossed across my breasts, hoping she would look away.

Finally, she asked Buaji, between mouthfuls of hing kachori, 'How old is our Srilaa now? Old enough … ?'

Buaji offered her sweetened lassi with a thick layer of fresh malai. 'Old enough for what exactly?'

The aunt responded, 'She has matured since I last saw her. I can tell from the way her body is developing,' gesturing, her hands waving and flapping in front of her own heaving bosom.

Buaji was conscious of the maharaj standing close enough to the table to overhear and see the aunt's hands clearly. 'Maharaj,' she said firmly, 'please go to the kitchen and get fresh kachoris.'

The kitchen was on another floor. He'd take about eight minutes to return. She asked me whether I wanted to go to my room and finish my homework. I protested saying I wanted fresh kachoris, too.

The aunt chortled, 'Let her stay ... after all we are discussing her future.' Buaji tried to shush her, but the aunt would have none of it. Turning to me she said, 'I have seen a very nice rishta for you ... he's a good boy from a decent family in Raipur. Next year, he will complete his education. The year after that, he wants to settle down with a girl from an equally well-placed family. Your Babuji is in steel. His family is in minerals. You will be very well looked after. Only son!'

Buaji was staring at me intensely, as if to gauge my reaction. I looked stonily at my thali and wondered why the kachoris were taking time. Buaji asked what had happened to the maharaj ... had he suffered a stroke on the way to the kitchen?

The aunt continued, 'I told you what a fine family it is—the pride of Raipur. They have built a school, hospital and temple. All they wanted was a bahu from a known family. And why tell lies? They want a fair girl. Very fair. Like you. Your complexion is what they are looking for in their bahu. You will live in the lap of luxury, my dear. You will be treated like a maharani, nothing less. How many servants do you want? Ten? This family will give you twenty. Bas. No dowry, nothing.'

I said, 'Where is my kachori? I want kachori.' And burst into tears. Not muffled sobs, but noisy tears. Buaji got up from her chair and came towards me. She touched my upper arm lightly and gave it a slight shove. 'Go and wash your hands … I will send the kachoris to your room with Chumki. Go!' I rushed from the long and grandly decorated dining table, with silver thalis and glasses and katoris gleaming under the large central chandelier. Suddenly, a room I always loved for its space and bright lights, had shrunk and turned dingy. I felt there were snakes crawling under the table and rats scurrying around, while raucous crows had the temerity to fly in from the balcony and help themselves to the half-eaten, cold, stale kachoris strewn all over the starched lace, hand-embroidered table cloth.

When I entered my bathroom, I was shivering even though it was the height of summer, and my teeth were chattering. Just the way they used to when I was three or four years old, and had wet my bed but was too scared to wake up Chumkididi. She would inform Buaji the next morning, and I would be reprimanded for behaving like a baby. Well, I was a baby. Still. I didn't want to grow up. Grow older. Grow breasts. Bleed. I was not done being a child. Why were they all after me to become a 'woman'? I didn't want to meet this boy from Raipur or any other boy. I didn't want to leave my home. What rubbish was that horrible woman talking! Rubbish!

I caught sight of my face in the bathroom mirror. I was bent over the basin doing what I was instructed to do non-stop—wash my hands. I looked closely at my face. That aunt said I was fair. Very fair. What did that mean? I stared at the skin on the inside of my arms, just below my armpits. I could see thread-like, spidery veins just under the surface, over the muscle. I looked at my feet—I had curled my toes, just like I used to when I was two and could not hold my urine any longer. What are these people talking about? Are they mad? Bahu—me? I don't ever want to get married. Ever. I want to stay a child. I will speak to Buaji when she's free.

That talk didn't really go the way I wanted. When I met her, she was busy with the kitchen staff, planning what to serve for Babuji's annual Diwali party for his friends and customers. Ma used to attend the dinner, but not participate as such. Sometimes she would have a headache and stay in bed. Sometimes she would leave for her social work just before the guests arrived. It was always left to Buaji to do everything. I would, of course, be given five sets of new clothes—one, for each day of Diwali. Chumkididi would be most excited to dress me up, fussing over each tiny detail. The jewellery for each occasion would be selected by Buaji, carefully removed from the gigantic tijori on our floor, placed in satin pouches resting on an old silver thali, carried by a trusted family retainer to my room, with Buaji bustling behind him, keeping an eagle eye on his every step and move.

Buaji was in the store room, when I agitatedly asked to speak to her. She turned around calmly and said, 'Later ... not now.' The 'later' came a week later. By then I had half-forgotten what I wanted to say. So, in a silly rush, I blurted out, 'I never want to get married! I hate men.'

She smiled, called me closer, and buried my face in her ample bosom. 'Have a laddoo. Freshly made. Your favourite ... besan. I personally sat with the servants when they were adding ghee to the kadhai. Come on ... what is there to cry? Who is getting you married tomorrow morning? Nobody! But remember, in our community, the good boys are taken by the time they are eighteen. And good girls are booked when they come of age. You have come of age now ... if we agree to the alliance, I am sure the boy's family will wait till you finish school. Things are different these days. At least, nowadays we inform the girls beforehand. In my time, we were pledged to the boy's family without anybody telling us! That is how my marriage happened!'

I cried out without thinking, 'But Buaji ... I don't

want to be you!' She was silent. Then she turned away and asked the servant whether the maharaj had remembered to order pista-badam for the barfis.

~

On my fifteenth birthday, I met my future husband for the first time. He was quite nice, actually. Such boys used to be described as 'tall, dark and handsome'. Ruchir from Raipur (I always thought of him as that—Ruchir from Raipur, was quite tall, not all that handsome ... but definitely dark. Like polished ebony. His eyes were magnetic. And he had a dazzling smile which showed his white, perfect teeth. His manner was easy ... you know? Confident and relaxed. Extremely rich boys are often like that. Money gives them a glow. I wanted to stare and stare at his face and body, but Buaji had warned me to keep my eyes lowered.

'It is not proper to make full eye contact at the first meeting. Later on, once the rishta is pucca, you can look openly and even talk to the boy. But not at the first meeting.' Ma was present when Ruchir from Raipur arrived with his family in a cavalcade of six cars—three imported, three Indian. He got out of a Mercedes with his maternal uncle and mother. He glanced up at the window from where I was peeping, with Chumkididi holding my shoulders tightly. She had been beside herself with excitement while dressing me up, fussing and fussing and fussing.

Ma had come in to take a final look. Thank God, I had passed her scrutiny! She smiled and hugged me, saying sweetly, 'My little dolly ...' She was looking stunning herself, in a floral French Chiffon saree, three lines of pearls, diamond clips from her mother ... I think they were Cartier, and her favourite Golconda ring. Her hair was neatly coiffed, and not left wild and open (I preferred her wild hair), and she had applied lipstick—this was unusual for her.

Babuji, was looking stylish and wonderful in a biscuit-coloured linen suit, open at the throat, burgundy-coloured loafers, and navratna cuff links from the family jeweler in Jaipur.

Buaji ... well, she was Buaji. Always impeccably turned out, but I did notice she was wearing her emerald strands after ages, and an emerald ring, along with her everyday diamond rings.

Chumkididi was dressed in a purple saree with a gold border, and it suited her a lot! As for me, I wore what Buaji had commissioned from our family weavers in Banaras—a delicate ice cream pink saree with a dull gold tissue blouse. She had said it would enhance my complexion and make me resemble a rose in full bloom. My jewellery was kept to a minimum ('Girls from our family should not come across as show-offs. In-laws get worried if the girl wears to much jewellery ... they start imagining her demands after marriage.') I was instructed to wait in my room, until I was summoned.

Fortunately, Buaji did not ask me to serve tea. She knew how clumsy I was, and it would have been a social disaster had I spilt tea on Ruchir from Raipur. For twenty minutes, I stared at my pedicured toes and admired the shell pink polish on my toe nails ('A woman's feet must look pretty at the first meeting. Elders always check the feet first. Any birth defects? Is the big toe shapely? What about the second toe! Longer than big toe—ufffff—the girl will dominate her husband.') I didn't like my feet all that much. But after twenty minutes of staring hard at them, I felt I had fallen in love with my toes.

'Which subject do you most enjoy in high school?' The feet-spell was abruptly broken by a male voice. I was the only school girl present. The question must be to me, I reasoned, and looked up. All eyes were on me. Except Ma's. She was staring out of the window and her eyes were closed. The voice belonged to Ruchir from Raipur, who was looking at me curiously. He seemed sympathetic. I said swiftly, 'History.' It was a big, fat lie. I hated history. In fact I hated all subjects. I hated school, too.

He nodded and said, 'Interesting. Which period in history is your favourite?' Without hesitation I replied, 'Moghul'. I knew nothing about the Moghuls, except that one of the emperors had built the Taj Mahal. Buaji intervened and asked, 'More chai, anyone? Our maharaj adds green cardamom while brewing tea—it's very good for health.'

Ma suddenly spoke, as if she had awoken from a trance, 'Cardamom gives me a migraine. Actually, nearly everything gives me a migraine.' Babuji got to his feet and said gently, 'My wife has been feeling a little under the weather. It's the humidity in Kolkata. It triggers all kinds of allergies. Come, my dear … you need to lie down and rest.' Ma blew me a kiss and whispered, 'Bye, my pretty polly-dolly …' That said, she was gone.

But Ruchir from Raipur stayed. And stayed. He asked Buaji if he had her permission to escort me to the garden just beyond the porch. A distance of two hundred metres. No more. She nodded her assent. Babuji had come back briefly, excused himself and left. It was just us—Ruchir from Raipur, his family, Buaji and me. Our garden was Buaji's pride and joy. She knew every shrub and tree. Babuji had his favourites, too. I loved the champak, with its gnarled branches and fragrant flowers.

As we self-consciously left the adults, feeling their eyes on our retreating backs, I said, 'I hate school. I hate studies. I don't mind getting married immediately and not appearing for my finals.'

Ruchir from Raipur laughed, 'So … that's what marriage means to you? No exams? Why do you hate your school so much?'

I walked towards the champak tree and spoke to it, not him. 'I don't have friends. My teachers are horrible. I find the studies very boring.'

He paused before saying, 'What if we enrolled you

in some other school and you could choose your own subjects? I am sure my parents won't object.'

I let out a small squeal, and jumped into his arms, my eyes shining with excitement. 'Really? Promise?'

He nodded, 'Promise.' We walked back together. Both of us were smiling. Buaji came up to me and asked softly, 'You like the boy? Shall I inform your Ma and Babuji?' I nodded my head vigorously.

But something terrible happened before our marriage date was set. I had sex with a stranger. And I was no longer a virgin. Which meant Ruchir from Raipur would not be getting a virgin bride, as was the agreement, without it being a proper agreement. But it was understood. And I realised I had put Buaji in the worst possible situation by telling her what and how it all happened. She would now have to take Babuji and Ma into confidence.

Chumkididi knew, of course. Chumkididi always knew everything, our relationship was such. She had wailed and wept for hours when I told her about it. 'Buaji will say it's all my fault. I suppose it is. I should not have left you alone with that devil. But I didn't know you would be all alone with him.'

Chumkididi didn't understand one important thing: I was not complaining! I only wanted to share what had happened with Amit, my cousin's boyfriend. Just share. No guilt or anything. I had enjoyed whatever Amit did to me. It was mutual and I had helped him to undress me, when he couldn't unfasten my bra quickly enough.

He had also fumbled with his own shirt buttons, and I had quickly done the job for him. I wanted to see his chest, the colour of his nipples. He said he also wanted to see mine. I showed him whatever he wanted to see or examine more closely. What is there to feel ashamed of? He said we would have to do it really fast, before my cousin got home from her tennis match (she lost that day).

He stared at my body and commented, 'Your tits are huge! Much bigger than hers!' That made me feel nice! She was always and always comparing, and saying things like, 'Such a pity you don't play any games, Srilaa ... you should, you know ... look at my legs and look at yours.' Now I would be able to say, 'Look at my breasts and look at yours.' Anyway ... Amit entered me pretty roughly after spending half a minute licking my nipples.

He did not kiss me. I really wanted to kiss him, so I held his face in both my hands and forced him to open his mouth. He pushed me away and said, 'Idiot!' I didn't care. His chest was good, but I didn't like the stubble on it.

Midway through his thrusting, I asked, 'Why do you shave your chest hair?' And he got angry. 'You really are an idiot! Why don't you just shut up? My focus is getting spoilt.'

So, I kept mum and soon it was over. I wanted to use the bathroom and wash off all that stickiness, but he said, 'She will be here any minute ...' He threw my clothes at me, got into his clothes and lit a cigarette. He did not offer me a puff. I really wanted to try a cigarette. I rushed out of my cousin's home, greeted her servants, and got into my car, where Chumkididi was waiting (I was not allowed to leave our home without Chumkididi).

She looked at my disheveled state and asked, 'What did you do to yourself?'

I smiled and shook my head, 'I didn't do anything ... Amit did this to me?'

She was about to scream, but checked herself, 'Amitbhaiyya? Sanjuktadidi's boyfriend? What was he doing there when she was not home? He fought with you?'

I laughed, 'Not exactly ... but he took my clothes off and we did that!'

I thought Chumkididi would faint. Her eyes widened and she whispered, 'THAT? No! Are you sure it was that?' I nodded my head and confirmed it was that. She started to cry. 'What will I tell Buaji?' Chumkididi said Buaji. Not Ma.

I replied casually, 'Say nothing. What is there to say? It is over, na?'

Chumkididi lowered her voice so that the old family driver couldn't hear what she was saying next, 'What if Ruchirbhaiya finds out? He may cancel the wedding.' I was hungry and wanted to eat puchkas and jhaal muri. I had not paid much attention to what she was saying.

I touched my breasts proudly and announced, 'I

think he really liked my breasts! He said how huge they were ...' The driver heard. I know he did. His eyes met mine in the mirror. He kept driving like he was deaf. Ma had trained all our drivers very well. They were to pretend to be deaf and dumb at all times, no matter what was happening in the back seat.

Chumkididi was wiping her sweaty brow with her saree pallu and looking nervously at the traffic whizzing past our old Merc—Babuji's favourite one. I told her, 'Don't worry ... I will tell Ruchirbhaiya everything myself.' And I did just that.

'I have done something terrible,' I told him when he came over to show me the watch he had bought as a gift for me. A beautiful Piaget in white gold, with tiny diamonds on the bezel. He asked, 'Did you murder someone? If yes, who?'

I was still staring at the Piaget and trying to fit it around my wrist with his help. The watch was distracting me. So, without bothering with how I phrased it, I said lightly and conversationally, 'Oh ... I had sex with Amit. You know Amit ... my cousin Sanjukta's boyfriend? He plays squash at the club with you sometimes ... same chap.'

Ruchir from Raipur froze. The strap of the Piaget was still in his hand as he tried to help me with the clasp. He said, 'Oh ... Amit ... yes.' That was it. I waited for a bit, expecting a reaction. He said, 'Glad you love the watch ... I bought a matching one. We can wear them together at the reception.'

Finished. Nothing more. I looked at the Piaget and said emotionally, 'It's so gorgeous! I love it.' He nodded. I had not had sex with him. And wasn't planning to, till our wedding night. But with the watch gleaming and twinkling on my wrist, I felt like it. So I asked, 'Why don't we also have sex? Right now? I quite enjoyed it.'

He replied, 'Okay … Where?'

I pointed to my bedroom, 'There … you will like my bed. It is so comfy!'

I am not sure what I felt about becoming a 'non-virgin'. Or whether I really, really enjoyed sex. Ruchir from Raipur was quite an expert, I discovered to my delight. Far better than that oaf, Amit. My ugh cousin deserved him, and he deserved her. My future husband seemed to enjoy my body almost like a man on an expedition, discovering new caves. I was flattered by his enthusiasm and responded with my own curiosity. I had never seen a naked man till that Amit encounter. And that afternoon, there had been no chance to examine a male body in the way I was keen on. He had barely undressed, such was his impatience to enter my body.

Ruchir from Raipur was not in a hurry. And he was surprisingly relaxed about every aspect of our intimacy, including my minute scrutiny of his scrotum. 'Do all balls look the same?' I asked, holding his like they were two ripe jamuns.

He smiled, 'Do all breasts look the same? Stupid question. Next!'

I made him lie on his stomach, and climbed over him to take a better look at his buttocks. I was silently running my palms systematically over his back and examining the moles on his shoulders. I let my fingers linger over a scar on his upper arm. And then traced my way over to his upper thighs.

He did not object when I reached between his legs. 'Your thing is so funny from this angle!' I exclaimed. 'So is yours ... have you ever seen it closely?'

I confessed I had tried positioning Ma's compact with a shiny mirror and a small light for her to touch up her face in the car, in a way to look inside myself. But the experiment was a flop. Ruchir from Raipur offered to show me how I looked down there, by propping me up on the edge of the marble, old-fashioned bath tub in my bathroom.

I politely said, 'No, thank you ...' and there our love making ended, but not before I asked him if he wanted pakoras and samosas and jalebis, which I could smell, as the Maharaj prepared the daily evening nashta for Babuji, and whosoever was at home.

He declined and added, 'I would prefer a smoke.' I pointed to the smaller balcony at the back of my bedroom, and said, 'You can smoke there ... nobody will see you.' 'Naked? Like this?' he wondered aloud. I nodded, 'Like this ...'

Our ritual was set. And nobody thought to ask any questions. We were engaged. My future husband had the exclusive right over my body from this point on. I didn't mind. Honestly speaking, it suited me fine. Chumkididi would pretend she had urgent errands to attend to on the other side of the mansion, and return only when Ruchir from Raipur's shiny black Buick drove out of the porch. Buaji pretended she had not noticed a thing. But of course she had!

I knew because of her instructions to Maharaj to make a selection of delicacies for 'Chhotey Babuji' every afternoon; whether or not he touched a single item on the silver salver. I found it odd ... or maybe not so odd, that Ma made no mention of my fiancé or even asked what I felt about the impending nuptials. She would look at me dreamily and sigh, 'My pretty dolly ... my baby girl ... life is changing.'

So it was! And I was in a bit of a trance, only waiting for the afternoon trysts with Ruchir from Raipur. I was getting used to his body being a part of mine. He had become like my favourite blue duvet with the tiny pink flowers. He had started to smell like it too, a heady but oh-so-familiar combination of so many aromas—Ma's Arpege (which I always 'borrowed' before our trysts), my own sandalwood oil, a touch of almond oil, a bit of that London soap Babuji always brought back for me. All this had now been mixed up with Ruchir from Raipur's aftershaves (always a combination of fragrances, never just one), and his own special body odour, which was not unpleasant.

'I feel jealous ... about you sleeping with other girls. Do you also feel jealous? You didn't react when I told you about Amit and me. Why? Most men are so stupid and possessive. Chumkididi had told me I was the biggest fool to tell you about Amit. She said you would break off the engagement and marry some other girl ...' All I got was a shrug. Funny fellow. In books and movies men always get very, very angry. Some even kill the woman, or the man, or both. But this fellow didn't seem to mind! Or care.

~

I repeated the question, but worded it differently this time. He looked at me and said flatly, 'Ask your Babuji where your Ma goes every afternoon, whom she meets. And you'll have your answer.'

I kept quiet and asked, 'Should I shave my pubic hair or wax it?'

Ruchir from Raipur grinned, 'Keep it! I like it.'

I knew Buaji had ordered tea cake from Flury's that afternoon. This seemed the perfect moment to share cake. I was beginning to fall in love with this chap. He didn't talk a lot, which was good. And he didn't overstay his welcome in my bedroom. Which was the best part. I liked being left alone after sex. And sex made me hungry. Even before he was done, I would start visualising the tea tray and imagine what else Buaji had ordered for us.

We had become 'us'. Even though nobody said so. And everybody pretended not to notice there was a large black car which did not belong to the family, boldly parked next to Babuji's. Sometimes, I would hear the drivers chatting softly amongst themselves. Despite that, it was as if a ghost visited me most afternoons, and a naked ghost was sometimes spotted smoking on the small balcony at the back of my room.

Late one humid, sweltering afternoon, after one of those Kolkata showers that drench the city for an hour, and disappear, I ran into Ma in the long corridor that led to her room.

She seemed pleasantly surprised to see me, and waved a tiny wave, 'Hello, my pretty dolly ... nice dress ... you might need a pedicure ...' she said in a rush and was about to enter her permanently darkened, cooled and fragrant room, when I stopped her and said, 'Ma!' There must have been a sense of urgency in my voice, which she sensed and stopped, her hand on the polished door knob.

'Yes, my little baby? Something wrong, darling?' I started stammering. Old nervous habit when in the presence of Ma. 'N-n-n-n-o! Just wanted to spend some time with you.'

She looked startled. Like I had suggested something entirely preposterous 'With me? How sweet, darling ...' She didn't say whether I could or couldn't.

But I persisted. 'Just five or ten minutes ... that's all.' She stared at her watch worriedly and kept silent.

I hastily backed off. 'It's okay, Ma. It's fine ... maybe some other time.'

She smiled a grateful smile. 'Sweetie ... definitely ... yes ... soon.' And she disappeared into her darkness. As she always had.

~

Ma was my biggest weakness. And the most troubling mystery in my life. Nobody wanted to provide any clues when I asked even simple questions. The answers used to be studiedly vague and evasive. Buaji's starched and controlled expression used to change at the mention of Ma. Chumkididi would look at me beseechingly and say, 'I know nothing!' Asking Babuji was not an option. I desperately wanted to know—everything—or even a little. There was a portrait of Ma, painted by some famous artist. I would gaze into her expressionless eyes, and try and find a clue or two. There was also an ornate silver frame with her wedding photograph. She looked beautiful, in a tragic sort of way ... a little betrayed and lost. She was sixteen or so at the time. Like I was at my betrothal.

I looked rebellious but happy in my engagement picture. Maybe I was still thinking of the kachoris I didn't get to eat! But Ma? She looked like a she-goat being led to the slaughterhouse. Babuji looked proud and stately. When did this fragile, delicate beauty turn into a

'Madamji'? And why? I could hardly enquire with Ramlal, the oldest driver in service. He used to drive Babuji to school. There were pictures of them in Darjeeling, with Babuji seated on Ramlal's shoulders.

My father was a sharp-featured, aristocratic looking man, who had been sent off to St Paul's, the posh and exclusive boarding school for children of the wealthy. The few friends he cared to spend time with were from that era, that school. 'I have nothing in common with these Marwaris, but one is forced to be polite at social functions. My friends prefer books to ledgers. They read ... hunt ... travel ... are more refined.'

Buaji discouraged such comments at the table—the rare times he would join us. 'Don't forget your own Marwari roots,' she'd say. And then swiftly change the subject. Ma was considered 'different' (for want of a better word). She didn't conform to any known stereotype. Buaji once told a visiting great aunt, 'Madamji is trapped in her own beauty ... I feel sorry for her. Beauty can be such a cruel prison.'

I didn't understand what she was saying. Ma was perfection to me. Nothing but. How could her beauty harm her? Babuji had married her for that very same beauty! He was the biggest catch of his time. And he had chosen Ma over all the other alliances that came from far and wide.

'Even England and Uganda ...' Buaji had once boasted, looking proudly in Babuji's direction. Ma, some said, had 'saved' her family by agreeing to marry Babuji. Her father had lost a great deal of money in the cotton trade and was heavily in debt. Babuji's father had stepped in to bail him out ... in return for his daughter's hand in marriage to his Oxford-educated, handsome son.

'She will bear him many sons ... and she will be the Lakshmi of our home,' he had prophesised. Well, the rest of the story did go according to plan, but Ma did not, and could not bear Babuji the much-valued son. She barely managed to deliver her first and only child—me. Her health was never the same after that, and Babuji was never the same with her, either.

The floor which had been readied for Ma after her stay at her maternal home, post-delivery, was the floor she chose not to move out of. It was a clear choice, and perhaps Babuji was relieved. Their life as husband and wife ended within the first year of marriage, and unfortunately, they never became friends.

Babuji's floor was out of bounds to all of us. The chances of Ma and Babuji even running into one another were pretty remote. He had his set routine, and she had hers. Babuji played bridge and golf, she was engaged in 'social work'. Babuji met his few old friends at the club, and she met nobody that I knew of. He went for a daily swim, and then a walk around the golf course. Twice every day she liked to get a massage with freshly pressed almond oil. Their instructions to the kitchen staff were precise and different. Babuji preferred what was called

'Conti' food at night. Strictly vegetarian, of course. Ma made do with light soups and grilled vegetables. Despite the well-established eating habits of those two, Buaji ordered a full Marwari meal twice a day, with elaborate snacks in between.

'Food is culture,' she would say. 'We are known by the food we eat and serve our guests. This mansion has an old tradition which goes back sixty years. Our kitchens were legendary. Some of our family's specialties came with secret recipes. Our cooks impressed the British guests who dined at that long, mahogany table ... the memsahibs would ask for second helpings! No, my dear, such traditions have to be maintained at any cost.'

I suppose so ... even though there was nobody to relish those meals. I had carelessly commented, 'Buaji, what a waste!'

She had turned to me sharply and said, 'Nothing is ever wasted. Marwaris don't waste—it's our biggest strength. We put a value on each and everything. Waste is considered a paap. Money is precious. Marwaris have known what it is like to survive droughts. But we have always survived! We can eat thorns from the desert—but we won't starve.'

~

Buaji was always right. I knew that. When she told me stories about our ancestors, her eyes glistening at the memory of their heroic deeds, I would feel my chest filling with pride. It was true. Marwaris were survivors of the hardiest kind. Which is why we could move here there and everywhere, not just in India but across the world. We worked hard and we succeeded. Then why did people call us stingy? I grew up listening to barbs like, 'kanjoos-makkhichoos'. So silly! Why compare us to 'makhkhis'? Were we no better than flies sitting on mithai and sucking up sugar syrup?

Even our Bengali neighbours were mean to us. 'These people smell of khatta dahi. Uffff! Do they eat it all day? Or do they smear it all over their bodies?' Such mean comments. Though, I admit Ruchir from Raipur did leave behind a rancid yogurt after-smell. I wanted to ask those superior, snooty Bongs, 'What about your sarson-ka-tel odour? Who applies stinky mustard oil all over—even there?'

Behind our backs they called us, 'Those Maadus'. It seemed most unfair! I would also face the occasional taunt in school: 'Oh ... Srilaa ... try asking her for a treat, or to share her lunch box.' They used to be pretty mean to me at times. But I didn't let it bother me. I would watch the others greedily eating from each other's tiffins and I would walk away. Chumkididi would remind me to finish whatever was packed in my dabba, and I would do that, without wondering what the others were enjoying.

Buaji always said, 'Don't listen to other people. Listen only to your elders. Learn from them. Had you been born a boy, Babuji would have started taking you to his office while you were still in your pram!'

I had asked Babuji once to take me to his office so I could sit in his big car. He had laughed and said, 'Offices aren't for girls. You stay home and learn embroidery from Buaji if you feel bored.' He had probably not noticed or pretended to ignore angry tears streaming down my flushed cheeks. I used to wonder if Babuji had ever seen me—*seen me*, you know? Properly. Did he know my left eye was smaller than the right one? Or that I had lost my front teeth as a child after falling off the guava tree in the garden behind our mansion? Did he know what I liked to eat? Which food I avoided? Well, neither did Ma. I was used to it.

~

Ruchir from Raipur also never asked me the sort of questions I wanted to answer. Once I enquired, 'Do you like my inner thighs or outer thighs?'

He looked at me and said, 'I don't know. I don't think about your thighs.' I felt that was an insensitive answer. I knew the difference between his inner and outer thighs. I also knew his one testicle hung lower than the other and was considerably smaller. I had mentioned it and he'd got most annoyed.

'You talk such nonsense, Srilaa. It's childish and silly to mention such things. I am going to be your husband soon ... we cannot behave like children.' I didn't know what to discuss with him. Once I asked him whether he'd been to the Arctic Circle. My Geography teacher had given us an interesting project on it. He didn't bother to reply, but reached over and touched my nipples instead. Such a strange man to do that, when I wanted to talk about the ice cap and all that. Another time, I brought up Amit and my first sexual experience. I wanted him to share it with me. What's the point of marrying someone if you cannot share everything and anything with them?

He turned his face and crinkled up his nose. I persisted. He gave me a slap. Really! A tight slap. Why? I tried to slap him back. But he caught hold of my wrist and twisted it hard. Hard enough for me to squeal in pain. 'Idiot, saali!' he spat out. Adding, 'You are lucky I am still marrying you. Spoilt bloody maal. If my family ever finds out you are not a virgin—khatam! Marriage off. Understand, kutti?'

Actually, I didn't understand! What was there to understand? What was so great about being a virgin? Sex is sex. If not Amit, it would have been some other boy. That's all. And what actually happens during this great 'sex' people talk about? A man puts his penis inside you for a few minutes. What else? It feels nice sometimes and not so nice sometimes. Why does everybody create so much drama over something so simple? I liked sex. It made me feel good. I liked my body. It looked quite beautiful in the mirror. Sometimes, while staring at myself in the mirror,

I would feel some tingling sensation and that also felt good. I would lean towards the mirror and kiss myself all over. Once or twice Chumkididi had walked in and seen me. She had scolded me for nothing and made me stop! Anyway. From the day Ruchir from Raipur slapped me for asking an awkward question, I decided not to talk to him. I mean, about personal matters. It was better this way. We would only discuss food. He liked rasmalai and so did I. After sex, we would enjoy a bowl of rasmalai and lick our lips. Sometimes, he would drop some between my breasts and lick it off, slurping like the neighbour's huge tom cat which drank milk so noisily that he'd scare away the small parakeets in the jamun tree. I asked my husband-to-be whether he too wanted to scare away the parakeets, but he didn't understand.

One day, he ran straight into Ma when he was slipping out of my room. She smiled sweetly and asked, 'Do you take sugar in your tea?' I was used to her questions, but Ruchir from Raipur was stumped and embarrassed. He started to stutter, after diving to touch her feet to show respect.

She stepped back, startled and said, 'Oh no ... dear boy. Take care of your back ... you may sprain it.'

She leaned forward and caressed his cheek, 'Do remember to use protection ... it's important. Or so people insist ...' With that said, she wafted away, melting into the dark shadows of the unlit corridor.

He turned to me and asked in a perplexed voice, 'Was she talking about condoms?'

I shrugged. 'Could be. She said "protection", right? Could be anything—condoms or guns. No idea.' Ma was like that, and I wondered whether he was attracted to her ... she was mysterious, alluring, beautiful and fragrant. Everything I was not.

One day, if and when I mustered up sufficient courage, I planned to ask her if she liked men ... or women ... or neither. I wanted to ask Ma a thousand questions all in one go. But I knew her answers would be compressed into a single line, without any connection to what I had asked. I would be happy even with that! I was needy in a sickening way. And I used to dream of my mother more than I dreamt of anybody else. Sometimes, she'd be naked in my dream, sitting by the window in the music salon, staring at the neem tree and singing softly to herself, oblivious to the constant parade of servants passing by her to go to Buaji's room in the far corner. They would also ignore her, as if it was normal to see the lady of the house sitting by the window without a stitch on. Sometimes, Ma would be my child, and I her Ma. Her head would be in my lap, she'd be gurgling happily while I ran my fingers through her hair and stroked her brow.

These days I wanted very much to discuss sex with Ma. Was I doing it right? Did Ruchir from Raipur really enjoy entering me? Should I have waited till we were married before going to bed with him? What if I got bored with sex ... imagine, having sex with just this one man? Would my husband mind if I tried out other men? I was very sure I would not mind if he slept with other girls ... had already slept with dozens, would sleep with many more in the future.

It seemed perfectly natural to look around and find out what one enjoyed the most. I thought of sex as a mithai ki dukaan ... so much to choose from. Can't sample everything in one lifetime. Sweet, and savoury also. I preferred namkeen. Ruchir from Raipur liked meetha. He was a gulab jamun eater and I loved spicy puchkas, with that teekha paani flowing out of the corners of my mouth. Mithais in Kolkata are seasonal, unlike in the rest of India. Sandesh is not just sandesh all the year round. There are countless varieties of sandesh to choose from depending on the weather and one's mood. Nolen gur-er sandesh in particular. It has a short shelf life and is available for a few weeks. It has to be consumed fresh and cannot be stored.

I felt that way about sex. It had to be savoured and enjoyed like nolen gur. Or jalebis in winter. With hot tea drunk out of earthenware kullhads—easily disposable. Visiting a mithai shop is never a casual experience. First comes the anticipation—what to consume. Then the visuals. Followed by all the aromas: pure ghee, malai, pista, burnt milk, cardamom, rose petals, saffron, honey, sugar syrup, hung curd, cashews ... forget about sampling anything. This was already too much to absorb. Once the tongue got involved, the whole experience was transformed to a dance inside the mouth. To really,

really appreciate mithai, I believed one had to shut one's eyes, plug the ears and focus entirely on what the fingers were transporting to the waiting mouth. Once inside the moist and dark cavern, the teeth and tongue had to be left alone to do their job. No rush. No impatience. No immediate swallowing of even the tiniest morsel. A slow, slow, slow approach was the best ... gently nibbling and chewing, and lingering over each bite, while visualising what would appeal to the senses next. A longish pause, before starting all over again ... and then strolling over to the next mithai shop.

I often wondered whether Babuji had ever been to a mithai shop. Or did the mithai just present itself to him on demand? Ma? Was she the entire mithai shop herself? Or an indifferent sampler of delicacies and specialties meticulously laid out for her?

~

I was told by Buaji that I would be "trained" for marriage, now that the betrothal had been formalised. What sort of training, I asked, while Chumkididi avoided my eyes and busied herself arranging silver nut crackers (Buaji's lovely collection), on a large silver salver which always stayed close to Buaji's marble temple in the corner of her suite of rooms.

Buaji did not answer directly. She said she had a certain plan, that included grooming lessons, table setting, social etiquette, the correct forms of address while in the presence of elders, appropriate clothing while relaxing in one's chambers, formal dressing for family occasions, how to cut fruit, which silver vessels to use while serving meals to the men folk, the proper care of personal jewellery, maintaining daily accounts, folding and storing sarees with the help of maids, placing meal orders with the kitchen staff keeping individual dietary restrictions in mind, getting to know the members of the husband's extended clan, including those living overseas, learning the art of making paan and homemade mukhwas, showing respect by bowing and joining hands in the traditional way each time the in-laws entered or left the room, touching the feet of elderly family members on a daily basis, just before the morning puja, seeing that the puja thali was never short of fresh flower garlands, agarbattis and prasad created by the maharaj at sunrise, bathing and wearing a morning saree before waking the husband, arranging his morning nashta and tea tray ... these were rattled off from the top of her head, as if she had memorised the manual in a past life.

I listened thoughtfully and attentively, without interrupting Buaji even once. She thought I may have fallen asleep, and shook my shoulder gently to check. I smiled sweetly and asked if I could stretch out next to her on the bed and read a book. She frowned and snapped, 'Book? What good will books do for you once you are a married woman? Forget books ... I have asked Chumki to teach you embroidery from tomorrow. And yes, I am asking our family's old music guruji to come and start classical music lessons for you. Oh … those days! When Sitara Devi was our house guest and performed for guests in the main drawing room. And Vilayat Khan became a close family friend.'

I often wondered: what happened to 'those times'? Why did nobody visit us any longer? Music? Not heard. Dance? Unthinkable. Chumkididi told me about how her mother, who used to work as a personal maid to Babuji's mother, had told her about the times there used to be garden parties with British saabs and memsaabs drinking tea on the lawns. Once there was also a proper 'ballroom' dancing party in the drawing room, which was almost as large as a school hall. Nobody went there these days. The furniture was covered, the heavy curtains permanently drawn. Once a year, an old chandelier cleaner would come to take down all the chandeliers—both big ones and small ones—and place them on the carpets, after making sure the carpets were covered with newspapers. Then, he would carefully dismantle each chandelier and start cleaning the crystals one by one. I used to sneak in and watch him for hours, as he hummed under his breath and continued polishing and polishing and polishing till the crystals started to steal the sun rays making their way past the small gaps in the curtain … creating hundreds of rainbows in the dark room. I would wait for the rainbows and start clapping gleefully pulling Chumkididi's saree and exclaiming, 'Look! So many pretty rainbows, Bhagwan is smiling at us ...' Then one day, Chumkididi told me the old man had died, and nobody else knew how to clean chandeliers. No more rainbows and no more smiles from Bhagwan.

I wondered about Ruchir from Raipur's home. I wanted him to show me photographs. I wanted to see what sort of a bed we'd be sharing. Was it as large as my four poster? As high? I still needed a foot stool to climb onto my bed. Did his bedroom have huge windows which opened out into the garden? He had mentioned a pet dog once. Did his pet sleep in the same room with the master. If so, I would be most embarrassed having sex in front of a dog. I started making notes in a small book which was placed on the bedside table. The notes were mainly about Ruchir from Raipur, with all the questions I needed to ask before we married. But he never gave me the chance to talk when we were together. He would brush me aside and say, 'Don't waste time ... take off your bra.'

I suppose this was how busy people managed so many things. So, I stopped wearing bras. To save even more time. But he got angry. 'Your breasts need the support of a bra,' he said, holding them up in both his hands like he was weighing melons before buying them. He remained in this position even after we had agreed I would resume wearing bras immediately. He said sternly he didn't want his wife's breasts to sag.

I also wondered about Chumki and her thoughts

on what was going on under her nose. Didn't Chumki experience sexual longings? Or didn't those matter, because she was 'only a maid' as Buaji often reminded me? That word defined Chumki's entire life. She was born a maid and would die a maid. And if she ever had a female child, that child would grow up to be my child's maid. And if she had a male child, he would become a driver or a durwan in our kothi. I had once argued with Buaji that Chumki should be given a day off occasionally, to just do nothing ... or do something. Anything. Buaji had sternly warned me not to get such funny ideas in my head. 'Chumki is happy. Very happy. She has a place to stay, food to eat, clothes to wear. Had she stayed in her village, she would have been raped ... and not just once. Without going to school, she would have had to work in the paddy fields, or be sent off to pick tea in one of the gardens. Here also, she would have been raped and thrown by the roadside. She is lucky to be in our home. We treat our servants very well.'

~

Just then, Chumki had walked in with fresh pomegranate juice for me. It was my mid-day juice time. Pomegranate or mosambi or nariyal. I think she had overheard the conversation. Chumki was not a snoop, she was always there. She couldn't plug her ears ... and I used to feel bad Buaji spoke about her as if she was invisible or stone deaf.

Chumki used to invent an errand in a different part of the mansion every time she spotted Ruchir from Raipur's car. She would wordlessly pick up a silver salver and say, 'It needs to be polished before Buaji scolds me.' And she'd swiftly disappear down the long corridor with its black and white checked marble tiles. If Ruchir from Raipur noticed her at all, he didn't reveal it. Once he was done, and finished with his smoke, I would spot Chumki waiting patiently at the end of the corridor. She would then walk up to me and utter the same word, 'Tired?' Once I asked, 'Why should I be tired?' She smiled, looked down and said, 'Men tire women.' I shot back, 'How would you know that?' And Chumki pretended to dust my bed and fluff up the pillows. 'I know men,' she answered quietly, and I thought, rather sadly.

Chumki and I shared a companionship based on loneliness. It worked for us. I had never seen Chumki unclothed, but she had seen me stark naked many times. Sometimes, when I was exhausted after sex, I would ask her to bathe me. She would fill the heavy gleaming brass bucket in my bathroom with hot water—really hot! And pour jasmine oil into it. I would be made to sit on a low wooden stool, shut my eyes and surrender, as Chumki poured near-scalding water on my over-heated body, singing softly, as she rinsed my hair, and scrubbed my back with a loofah. Sometimes, she would make me lie face down on my bed after the bath, and massage me, using talcum powder to better knead my taut muscles. I would often cry during the massage, hiding my tears from her by burying my face into the soft pillows and stifling my sobs. She would stroke my wet hair gently, then rub a gamcha over the strands spread limply over my back, before tying them up into a bun in the thin, checked towel. We didn't have to speak to one another. Everything was understood in the tenderness of the moment.

One afternoon, while Ruchir from Raipur was lying naked, sprawled against the pillows on my large, four poster teak wood bed, with its lion legs, his own legs spread-eagled, and a sad looking, flaccid penis wilting against his right thigh, Chumki walked in with my afternoon nashta and garam chai. I am still not sure if she did this deliberately, or she had not noticed the car downstairs.

~

At the time, I was seated in front of my dressing table, applying a new lipstick I had bought that morning. The shopkeeper had said it would suit my fair complexion and attract a good bridegroom. The thing is, Chumki did not look startled at this intrusion, as if it was natural to walk into a room and find a naked man on the bed. Moreover, Ruchir from Raipur wasn't startled either. He looked up casually without reaching for a cover, and indicated with a nod of his head that her presence had registered. She placed the tray close to his bare right leg, made eye contact, and walked out slowly, turning to look at me and say, 'Didi ... chai. Lemon ke saath.'

After that encounter, it no longer mattered to the three of us. And soon Chumki started offering a leg and head massage to Ruchir from Raipur—with oil and without oil. She also took to folding his discarded clothes and draping his shirt over the back of my chair near the window. He seemed relaxed and comfortable, asking her to instruct the cook to prepare his favourite teatime snacks, and to stock bottles of lemon barley in the fridge during the hot months.

I noticed Chumki had started dressing differently. Her body language too had altered. Each time she uttered the word 'Bhaiyya' (that's what the servants called my future husband—that, or 'Chhotey Saab'), she would glance sideways at me and blush. Chumki was falling in love with Ruchir from Raipur! I needed Chumki more than I needed him. Chumki was a habit. He was an indulgence. I didn't want to choose. And fortunately, I didn't need to. It was going along well, till one of the other servants—a senior maid who handled Buaji's personal work, like rearranging her cupboards regularly—carried tales to Buaji. I was summoned to her chambers by the senior maid, whom I detested, and she had the air of a sanctimonious government clerk who was out to get a junior sacked by sneaking on them. She walked ahead of me, her chest thrust out, her chin pointing heavenwards. I should have felt like I was being led to the guillotine, and would be asked my last wish before the noose tightened, but in fact, I felt nothing at all.

Buaji dismissed the maid and asked me to sit down next to her on the bed. I could see our reflection in the large mirror of the almirah. She asked desultory questions about my exams and tennis classes. And pointed to my feet saying the heels were chapped and rough. Tea arrived along with onion pakodas, papdi chaat and tea cakes from Flury's. I noticed the hand-embroidered napkins and matching tray cloth cover with bright red carnations in a corner. I complimented Buaji on the perfect tray setting as she watched me eat, her eyes never leaving mine.

She said, 'Babuji is not keeping too well ...'

I replied, 'Oh ... really? I had no idea! Does Ma know? Has the doctor seen him?'

Buaji avoided replying, she tasted the chaat and said, 'Not enough imli ... what is the cook doing these days? Not paying attention to his work. It is important for servants to know what their work is and focus on that. Most servants these days spend their time on other matters and ignore their work. Have you noticed, Srilaa?'

I ate some more chaat and said, 'I think the imli is fine.' Buaji took off her horn rimmed spectacles, adjusted her saree pallu and said, 'The doctor is coming tomorrow for Babuji ... and for you.'

I looked up with surprise, 'Why me?'

Buaji said evenly, 'To check just how much imli you are eating these days.' She knew! But who could have told her? Nobody else but Chumki. Bitch! Saali! Kutti! I would show her! I hastily got up and said, 'I have to finish a paper for tomorrow ... or else I will get into trouble.' Buaji said, 'You are already in trouble, my dear.'

It wasn't my fault! That Ruchir from Raipur was always in such a hurry. He refused to wear a topi, saying it made him lose his erection. I had argued, 'So your erection depends only on a condom ... not me?' He had ignored my remark and roughly entered me. It must have been the day Chumki had walked in and seen him lying naked on my bed. I missed my period fifteen days later and I remember Chumki asking me why I had not ordered extra sanitary pads that month. I always needed a packet and a half—ten were never enough, since I bled for six days. I had lied and said, 'This month I only needed nine.' She looked at me, paused and kept quiet. Next day, she served an extra portion of mango pickle on the thali. When I asked why, she said, 'In case you were craving something sour ...'

I started to hate her from that moment on. I pushed my thali away and said, 'I am not hungry. Go back to the servant's quarters and stay there till I call you.' She took her time to clear up and leave, adding, 'I can order samosas and sandesh for later ... Bhaiyya loves our house samosas. He was telling me that day ...' When could he have discussed samosas with Chumki? Didn't he always get into the car directly after leaving my room?

I decided to watch him more closely. The cigarette

smoking, the slow exit after a quick wash up in my bathroom ... maybe he lingered on the staircase and stopped in the small, dark alcove to catch his breath before climbing down the remaining stairs? I would time him and compare. Or, I would keep Chumki in the room till I heard his car leaving through the porch, and taking a turn onto the driveway, with the well-tended potted plants waving him goodbye. It was best to be alert around men. I had heard they could be very badmaash. Chumki had once said Ma was broken-hearted because of a badmaash man who had let her down. I don't think she was referring to Babuji. My father was not a badmaash. I think he was worse—he just loved money more and human beings less. He didn't care enough for people even to be a proper badmaash. Ruchir from Raipur resembled Babuji in many ways. His relationship with money was the only real relationship in his life. He didn't care if others recognised this trait.

'Come on ... I am a Marwari, yaar. How do you think we Marwaris have become this successful? It is because we worship Lakshmi. We never let her leave our home.' He had once looked at the small temple in my room and commented on the silver moorti of Lakshmi I had been presented by Ma during Lakshmi Puja, when I was twelve years old.

'Look after her well,' she had whispered, tugging her saree pallu nervously. I loved my Lakshmi and worshipped her every single day. Now this man was finding fault with her?

'Your Lakshmi is standing,' he pointed out reproachfully, 'which means she is ready to run out of the house. Lakshmi should always sit ... that too, with both feet tucked under her. So that she stays and makes herself at home. No wonder we are richer than your family. We have seated Lakshmis all over our house.' I stared at my beloved Lakshmi and started to cry. He thought I was being foolish and childish.

'Just change her ...' he said dismissively and left to smoke his cigarette. Even Lakshmi had watched us having sex. She knew everything. But she would never tell Buaji. Lakshmi loved me and I loved her.

Chumki brought me roasted papad to eat. This time with lime pickle and saunf on the side. I stared at her and asked sharply, 'What is all this nonsense? What is going on? Did I ask for papad?'

She smiled and said, 'No, you didn't. But I could sense you were longing for lime pickle. The doctor is coming tomorrow. Buaji told me to remind you.'

I found it hard to sleep that night. Of course, I knew the doctor would know. And I also knew he would tell Buaji and Babuji, perhaps Ma, too. I was not scared. I didn't think I had done anything bad or wrong. Ruchir from Raipur had been selected by them to be my husband. I had kept quiet. Got engaged. Now, I was preparing to marry him. He would have exclusive claim to my body sooner or later. Okay ... so, it was sooner. That's all. What could they say to me? Soon I would leave this home and move into another. I had already decided not to take Chumki with me to my new place. I would find another Chumki. Let them say whatever to me. I would tell them frankly it was all his fault for not listening to me and wearing a condom. I would tell him the same thing when he came to my room next: wear a condom or forget it. That conversation with Ruchir from Raipur never happened.

Two days after the doctor's visit, his maternal uncle, along with a family friend who was a well-known doctor, came to our home in the morning. They did not stay for naashta-paani. They went straight to Babuji's waiting room, where he met visitors. Ten minutes later, they came out briskly, got into their car and drove off. I saw Buaji rushing downstairs. Someone was sent to wake up my sleeping Ma and summon her. Nobody called me. An hour or so later, Chumki brought me a chilled glass of chhaas. She looked smug ... triumphant.

'Bhaiyya has broken off the engagement. I am not saying ... the servants and drivers are talking.' I turned to look at my Lakshmi. She had not left me. She was not going anywhere. She was not running away as Ruchir from Raipur had predicted. Lakshmi was going to stay. And she would be my best friend from that point on, I pledged to myself. I would make sure to love Lakshmi with all my heart for the rest of my life. I told Chumki to throw away that man's extra underwear and sports' shirts which were hidden behind my nighties in the top drawer of the cupboard.

'Won't Bhaiyya get angry if his things are thrown into the dustbin?' Chumki asked tartly. I tossed my head back and laughed, 'Let him get angry! Bloody son-of-a-sadela-bitch.' And then I asked her to get my tennis gear ready, and organise a warm mug of Bournvita.

Chumki muttered, 'What is the use of extra energy, now? Too late!' I exchanged glances with the Standing Lakshmi and said, 'It is never too late!'

~

'Baby ... forget it. Forget him. It wasn't your fault.' Ma looked like she was in a tearing hurry. Ma was always in a tearing hurry to go somewhere ... anywhere. She just didn't like being here. The parakeets were screeching louder than usual. I could hear the durwan's snores as Ma and I stood awkwardly in the passage, our eyes looking away ... at nothing.

'Lovely perfume, Ma,' I said. I really did not want to discuss Ruchir from Raipur anymore with anybody. I stared at my toes sullenly. Ma's glance followed. 'Chipped nail varnish, darling. Let me get my pedicurist to come home and pamper your feet. My treat!' Ma's treats were always odd. And at the oddest of times! The 'treat' I longed for was a conversation, not a pedicure. My feet didn't need pampering, Ma! It was my heart ... my insides ... my everything! I kept quiet and said, 'So sweet! Thanks, Ma.' She leaned over, as if to hug me ...

we were both embarrassed. She gave up and tousled my hair instead. 'Sex can be such a nuisance,' she pronounced with a nervous giggle as she looked for a quick escape. 'Bye, sweetie ... lots of kisses.'

I didn't see Ma after that brief encounter for what must have been weeks. I lost track of time and busied myself with activities I did not enjoy. I over-ate and kept dreaming about food. I had requested Buaji to replace Chumki as my personal maid. Fortunately, Buaji did not ask why. Chumki's duties were reassigned—she became a kitchen assistant and worked closely with Maharaj and his army, making sure meals and snacks were prepared and served on time.

Buaji did try and spend more time with me, especially after the 'procedure'—as the abortion was referred to. I don't recall too many details since I had been knocked out by the anesthesia. I could hear the doctors and nursing staff chatting casually, while they scraped out whatever remnants of Ruchir from Raipur were left inside me. A nurse asked, 'Why didn't they take the girl to London and have it done there? Most of the other girls go abroad for abortions ... some even deliver. This girl comes from a rich family, too. Why attract attention? People talk ... who will marry her after this?' Someone else added, 'But ... in their family, all this is chalta hai. You know about the girl's mother, I'm sure! It runs in the family. Chaalu mothers produce chaalu daughters.'

I think Buaji was bothered by the same problem—who

would marry me now that I was not considered 'intact'? She was already thinking ahead and planning the next alliance. I had seen two punditjis visiting her chambers armed with pothis and ganga jal for purification. One of them asked to spend time alone with the 'damaged' kanya. Technically, I no longer qualified as a 'kanya' since I had had sex and my hymen was broken. I was in nowhere land—neither a kanya nor a saubhagyawati. So, what was I? I agreed to meet the punditji in Buaji's ante-chamber.

He was a portly fellow clad in a diaphanous dhoti that was tucked tightly between his legs. So tightly, in fact, that it cradled his genitals snugly and his hairy buttocks peeped out each time he raised his stained, white kurta to sit down without crushing it. His small, close set eyes squinted at me as he said in a voice that was syrupy and low, 'Sab kuch theek ho sakta hai ... Bhagwanji ki kripa.'

I kept silent and focused on Buaji's heavy curtains with the pretty chintz print. He told me my future need not be jeopardised ... he was there to make sure I would get a good 'patidevta', despite my handicap. I told him I was not handicapped in any way, but he pretended he had not heard me. He leaned across and tapped my knee—the right one. His hand lingered more than I thought was appropriate. He smiled reassuringly and said, 'Ghabrao mat, beti.'

I felt a small shiver race up and down my spine, as I held his gaze and lied, 'I am not ghabrao-fied at all.'

He coughed and stared at Buaji's mandir, muttering,

'Durga! Durga!' Buaji glared at me and turned to the punditji, 'Srilaa is very upset ... any girl in her situation would be. We thought Ruchir was a good boy ... from a good family. Educated and khaandani. The servants also said the same thing ... he used to wish them nicely when he came in the afternoon to have tea here. God alone knows what bhoot got into him suddenly to pounce on our Srilaa that afternoon. Poor girl could do nothing with that rakshas. He had shut her mouth with his hand ... she could not scream or ask for help. Had the durwans heard her cry, they would have rushed upstairs and skinned that boy alive. His parents would have found his battered body ... nothing else. We are not vindictive people, punditji. We respect our women, our sisters and daughters. We could have gone straightaway to the nearest thaana and reported him. In two minutes he would have been arrested. But we decided our dignity was more important. Srilaa's izzat is worth more than such a scandal ... you know how people talk! Now we have to concentrate on her future, nothing else. Show us some good boys, punditji. Our beti's kundali is superb—filled with gold and riches, a life of comfort. She will bring so much prosperity to the home she enters as a daughter-in-law. We only care about her happiness. Bas.'

Punditji shifted his eyes from my face to my groin. 'But what do we do about THAT ...?' he asked waving his hand (the one with four gold rings, as he indicated my damaged vagina, the one that had no hymen left to protect my virtue).

Buaji said in an assured way, 'We will take care of that small problem, punditji. It is not such a big thing. These days girls are so active ... they go on cycles, ride horses, play tennis and all sorts of rough games. Small accidents happen ... I have already spoken to a trusted doctor. By God's grace, we can afford the best. If he cannot do it, we can go to London.'

I squealed, 'Let's go to London!' unable to conceal my excitement.

Punditji sighed, 'Yeh toh bilkul bachchi hai! She has not understood much.' How wrong they were! I had understood everything! If I was to get a new hymen, why not acquire it in London?

~

Ma was sent with me and Buaji to make sure I got my hymen back. Ma seemed somewhat distracted as she hardly spoke to either of us on the flight. I saw her drinking champagne and asked if I could take a sip from her flute. She smiled tiredly and replied, 'Sweetie ... you are young and beautiful ... you carry your bubbles within you.'

Buaji had covered her head with a mouse-coloured soft shawl and gone to sleep almost immediately. This was my first foreign trip and I wanted to share my enthusiasm with someone. So I started chatting with the purser and air-hostess who were both really friendly and kept feeding me salted almonds. 'Holiday?' one of them asked. Ma overheard and whispered, 'Not really ... we have to get my daughter fixed up ... you know? I'm afraid she has been a little naughty.' I didn't know I had been 'naughty'. What fun!

The purser excused himself and came back to offer Ma some more champagne. He said, 'I like naughty girls,' and winked at me. Ma caught that, and cooed, 'Sweetie ... get some sleep ... after all that afternoon activity, you should rest ... n'est ce pas?' Ma sometimes spoke in French which she said was almost as sweet as Bengali without Bengali's syrupiness.

The English doctor was soft-spoken and kind. He said he had performed my grandfather's hernia operation a few years ago. I thought, 'Oh well ... same region, so to speak. Below the waist and involving genitals.'

We were staying close to his clinic in a predominantly white neighbourhood. The doctor's nurse was from Jamaica and I instantly liked her. She stroked my hair and told me not to worry.

'He is famous for this particular procedure,' she boasted. And told me she had been around for at least thirty similar 'things'.

'Such an issue over a tissue,' she joked, adding it was only Indian, Arab and Pakistani people who bothered about such 'small matters' and paid so much to her boss to fix them. Buaji and Ma sat wordlessly in the waiting room. Ma looked different in London. Older and smaller.

Maybe because she wore trouser suits and closed shoes. I preferred her in sarees with pale roses printed on them. She wore her usual pearls and rings, ear clips and diamond bangles. I overheard Buaji telling someone over the phone that she was more worried about Ma than me, 'Srilaa is okay. But her Ma ... ?' As if Ma needed to get her 'thing' fixed. So stupid!

From her tone, I guessed she was talking to Babuji. I was happy he had asked about Ma and me. After the 'incident', as it was called, he had stopped talking to me. In fact, we hadn't met at all, except briefly, when I ran into him in the porch. He had nodded curtly and turned away. It had hurt me then. But not now. God knows what Buaji had told him about Ruchir from Raipur's afternoon visits. I am sure Babuji would have held Buaji responsible for not being strict enough with me.

But soon it was done! The 'thing' was out. And I was declared 'intact' again. The nurse commented playfully, 'Now your bride price can be doubled! Good investment.'

I didn't have the heart to tell her in India we buy grooms. Had I been talked about as not being intact down there, my family would have had to shell out an astronomical amount to the groom. Most Marwaris figure a one-time expense during the marriage works out cheaper in the long run than hosting an unmarried daughter in the father's home for life. Everything is worked out in terms of costs and expenses. Even marriage. This is one balance sheet Marwaris study the closest, since it is more than just a business decision. Once the girl is sent off to her new home, the hisaab kitaab is closed. A new ledger is rarely needed, unless, of course, there is a divorce involved. For Marwaris, this awful D-word is never uttered, much less considered. No matter what.

So, as I lay on that hospital bed, covered in a blue sheet, and very, very sore down there (peeing made me cry out in pain), I felt God had saved me from becoming Ruchir from Raipur's wife. I would have died as his wife. And the long years in between would not have counted at all. That Ruchir from Raipur's sperm was good enough to promptly fertilise my egg proved neither of us had a fertility problem. Had we married, I would have got pregnant on the honeymoon, delivered after nine months, then become pregnant again after two years ... and so on. Had the first child been a boy, there would have been no pressure to produce the second. I half-wondered what I had killed—boy or girl? I thought of a few names. Anupriya for a girl and Aparshakti for a boy. Maybe I had twins inside?

We got back from London after a month or so. I had lost weight. So had Ma. Buaji rarely stepped out since she felt cold all the time, no matter what the temperature indicated. A local Maharaj made our meals, but was a lousy cook. Ma sat by the window talking to the birds chattering on the branches of the tree near the window which looked out on the quiet street. She sipped warm water from a tumbler, and read or wrote in a leather-bound diary she'd remove from her handbag very carefully, as if not to hurt the pages.

Occasionally, she'd look at me and say, 'Sweetie … London can be most depressing … but then, so can Kolkata. Kolkata is even more depressing. Those filthy, crowded streets!' I would nod eagerly hoping to engage her in a longer conversation. But Ma would turn away and pretend to sing.

Once she asked, 'Would you like me to teach you the cha cha cha? It is very important to know how to dance the cha cha cha …' I jumped out of my chair and said, 'Please teach me, Ma!' By then, her mind was elsewhere. She was always sweet and kind, though, speaking softly about things I could not understand … almost as if she was having a conversation with herself, breaking into a girlish giggle from time to time.

By 7 p.m. she would retire to her room and I would hear music playing. Maybe she listened to the radio or watched television. I have no idea. I wish I had felt confident enough to knock on her door and walk in. She was like those tiny birds on the window sill which came looking for seeds and then flew away, disappointed. I wanted to feed Ma. And hold her close. I wanted to never forget her fragrance …

~

Back in Kolkata, I ran into a school friend at the club and she asked me about my broken engagement in a most natural way. As if it was perfectly acceptable to break off, when it wasn't. At first, I thought of lying and denying it. Then I thought to myself she would want to know if the wedding date had been fixed. Next, she would say, 'Show me your ring! How many carats?' Why were Marwari women obsessed with diamonds? This obsessed, I mean?

A lady who had come to meet Buaji kept turning her ring round and round and round on her finger, till Buaji was forced to make a comment. 'Have your fingers swollen? It happens in this sort of weather.'

The lady pretended to laugh and said, 'No Buaji ... I was just wondering whether the jeweler had done a good job of resizing it. Didn't want the stone to fall out ... you know what a 7-carat flawless costs these days! Of course, when Murliji gave it to me, it was much less.' Buaji looked dismissively at her and said, 'In our khandaan, we prefer ten carats and above ... but we never talk about it.'

Another time, I had met Ma's friends inside the smelly washroom of a cinema during the interval of a boring film, and overheard them discussing some other friend's fake diamonds. They had noticed me and said with a laugh as fake as the diamonds they were talking about, 'Don't mind us. We are only joking.'

Marwaris never joke about diamonds. Or money. I said, 'I didn't hear anything, aunties.'

They looked at each other and chorused, 'Aunties? How old are you, beti?' Strange. They were Ma's friends. Maybe the same age as her ... what should I have called them? I asked, putting on my baby voice.

They chorused, 'Call us GIRRRLS! Just girls. Or by our first names …' It was a valuable loo lesson. Some of my best lessons have emerged from bathroom conversations with strangers. I realised that day something far more significant about Ma. She was not like these women at all. Ma was different. She was her own woman. Ma was distinct and different. Not like other Marwari ladies of her age. Or any age. She never discussed diamonds. That made her unique.

I hung around taking time to wash my hands, listening to their animated chatter. The one wearing a mithai pink saree, with badly dyed hair was clutching the arm of the aunty in green embroidered chiffon.

'I asked my husband to increase the ghar ka kharcha allowance. He asked me to produce the kirana bills! Can you imagine? I said forget it, let everybody starve. So, he said who is starving? Not you, you fatty bambola! I started crying. He walked out of the room shouting, go and eat at your mother's house in Kanpur … then you will understand starvation.'

The green embroidered saree said, 'Forget it, yaar. All these bloody men are the same. As if we don't know what they spend on when they go on business trips to London? You should have said that, na? Not kept quiet? That's our problem. We keep quiet when we should open our mouths wide and give it back. Bloody ullus …'

I wondered if my Babuji was also a bloody ullu. I didn't think so. He did go to London and all that. I didn't know what he did there or how much he spent. Ma did not look into household matters. Buaji did that. So I never heard such talk in our home.

I had been bleeding heavily since my London trip. I had told Buaji and she kept promising to take me to some new doctor. I also felt something had changed down there. Especially when I peed. Or touched myself. I was used to touching myself since I was a child. I didn't know it was a bad thing, till Buaji told me to stop, when I was lying on the bed next to her and put my hand inside my knicker. It started with my scratching myself there, and then, it just carried on ... It felt really nice and tingly.

Suddenly, Buaji slapped my wrist sharply and said, 'Chhheeee ... what are you doing, Srilaa? Stop it, at once!'

I hastily withdrew my hand and asked, 'But why?'

Buaji searched for the right words and said, 'Because that part of a girl's body is dirty. Very dirty. It smells. If you touch it all the time, you will also smell and nobody will be your friend.'

I liked my own smell. But I kept quiet. Now after that London thing, I was wondering whether I had poked myself too hard and damaged something. These days I wasn't very enthusiastic to slip my hands into the elastic band of my panties. I tried a few other ways to feel the same tingling. But nothing worked. Maybe I was missing Ruchir from Raipur's fingers and touch ... howsoever rough. I was used to that. And had started to like it. Wait for it.

My broken engagement story was doing the rounds. People I was barely on 'Hello! Hello!' terms with, would come up to me, put on a sad face and say in a low voice, 'So sorry to hear about your engagement being called off. He was not a nice boy to do this to your family. We feel really sorry for your father. Terrible! No father should have to face this disgrace—imagine a daughter being rejected by the fiancé's family!'

Our society is also funny that way. Nobody gives any dosh to the boy. It is always the girl's fault. 'Don't feel bad, betey ... you will get another boy. Your family has good connections ... I know a boy who lives in Jamshedpur. Not as rich as your family. But decent background. Coal mines. Let me know if your family is interested in the alliance, okay, betey? Chalo ... see you.' And off went this uncle, with paan in his mouth, wiping the sweat off his brow. My lunch was ruined! I was planning to eat cheese sandwiches by the pool. And have a strawberry milkshake after. At our home sometimes the cheese sandwiches tasted of jhaal muree ... maybe the kitchen staff didn't wash their fingers before cutting the bread?

Another elderly lady accosted me near the pool, stared at my breasts and commented, 'We heard what happened. Tch tch tch ... very difficult. Men will be men ... but girls have to think about their family's izzat! Stay pure. Who likes stale food after another man has made the dish jhootha? In our family, we say, "Yeh ladki ab kaam se gayee". We feel bad for your Duaji. Such a fine lady. And you mother, of course ... but in her case, things are different. And I am surprised to see you swimming aaram se ... as if nothing's happened?'

I licked the orange popsicle in my hand, and offered it to her, 'Want? It is nice and jhootha!' She turned around and waddled off. Bitch!

It didn't end there. And I noticed the attitude of the staff had changed dramatically, too. The drivers had started giving me the eye in the rear view mirror. It was an insolent way of displaying their lack of respect for a girl who had let the family's honour down. The Maharaj cooked my favourite dishes most indifferently, and the durwan had forgotten to 'thoko' a smart salaam each time I entered and exited from the main gate. Even the gardeners would stop trimming the rose bushes and stare at me as if an alien had appeared in their midst. I noticed Babuji's staff looked at me in a strange way, not quite sure whether or not to acknowledge me. I wondered why my virginity or the absence of it, made such a difference to the lives of so many people! And how come everybody seemed to know exactly what was going on with my hymen! Was this a normal way to treat women? An elderly woman, maybe an old retainer's wife, came up to me, as I was about to enter my home, and whispered, 'A woman's womb is her temple ... nobody can enter that temple ... except when the seed is sanctified and pure. It is only a husband's adhikar to plant that seed. Our shastras are very clear, beti.' That said, and she shuffled off, wrapping Buaji's old shawl around her bony shoulders.

I ran into Babuji a month or so after my return from London. He stared at my face as if everything I had gone through was written on my forehead. He patted my head absently and asked, 'Would you like to go to Jamshedpur?'

I shook my head vehemently and said, 'No!' He nodded. And got into the car quickly. I rushed to Buaji's room. She was with a silversmith from Bora Bazaar—the same man who used to come to our home before Diwali each year and take orders for silver statues of Gods and Goddesses, which were sent out with boxes of mithai and dry fruits to Babuji's clients. She looked at me and may have sensed I was disturbed. She dismissed Kanhiyalal with a wave of her hand and told him to come back at the same time the next day. She asked for chilled coconut water for herself and Horlick's in hot milk for me.

I protested, 'I don't want milk, Buaji!'

She replied icily, 'We don't offer anything stronger to our children in this home.' Maybe Chumkididi had sneaked to Buaji about Ruchir from Raipur bringing a hip flask filled with whiskey for both of us—before and after we had sex. I blurted out, 'Buaji ... I hate milk. I prefer whiskey!'

She pretended not to hear what I had just said and said calmly, 'I have found a good rishta for you in Jamshedpur. I have the boy's photograph. He looks like Babuji. You will like him.'

I said, 'But I don't want to get married! I want to live

here forever ... with you and Ma and Babuji. This is my home.'

Buaji fiddled with her prayer mala of tulsi beads before replying in a measured tone, 'Srilaa ... this is not an ashram for rejected girls. You cannot live her forever. A girl has to go to her own home. She has to have a husband, a child or two. This is a temporary home. You are lucky we have found someone to marry you after what happened. I was sure his family would find out and cancel the meeting. But it seems they are open to it. Our family elder in Kolkata spoke to the boy's grandfather and convinced him about your character. He was told what happened was an act of pre-meditated violence. You were overpowered. You had no choice. Your mouth was stuffed with a soft pillow, while that man ... that man ...'

I said, '... fucked me. Yes, he fucked me very often. And you know what, I liked it a lot. I enjoyed myself. He didn't have to use force or stuff my mouth with anything.' I quickly added, 'If that Jamshedpur fellow asks me, I will tell him this. It is the truth.'

Buaji pounced on just one sentence—the last one! 'So, it is agreed! I will let the other party know. We can start planning for Jamshedpur.'

I looked out of her window where the cacophony of parrots had reached a crescendo. They looked so happy and carefree, chattering and eating and playing. 'I want to be a parrot,' I told Buaji and left her room. My mind was racing. I had heard Jamshedpur was the pits, from people in the club. Well, at the moment, my life was the pits, too! Maybe I would find even more parrots in Jamshedpur, and join them?

I ran into Ma, rather unexpectedly. She smiled, 'Sweetie ... you look happy! Are you well?' I wanted to hug her, and moved forward to do so. She stepped back nimbly and said, 'I am sweaty ... run along, dearest.' I started towards my room—my banishment chamber and called out to Ma over my shoulder, 'I want to be a parrot. In Jamshedpur.' She blew me a kiss and said, 'Lovely!' With that said, she was gone, in a blur of French chiffon.

My life as a parrot in Jamshedpur was about to begin. But before that, I had to end this Kolkata chapter. And I had a plan. I decided to write a letter to Ruchir from Raipur. It was important to let him know he was not a nice man. I knew it would make no difference to his life, but at least I would feel better. It was so easy to write down all those awful and not-so-awful memories once I started. It was like he was sitting across from me on that chair where he used to fling his clothes before having sex with me. The chair that still bore traces of one of our adventures, when it toppled over and the glass edge of the coffee table created a deep scratch on the leg. A scratch that was duly noted and reported to Buaji by the servant who was responsible for looking after my room.

When I wrote that five page letter, I visualised myself like a parrot. Like one of the parrots who would fly to our windowsill looking for remnants of seasonal fruits, especially guavas. I thought of myself as that parrot which had witnessed all our love making sessions and noticed many things. I convinced myself that parrots were observant and sensitive to human moods. So, I told Ruchir from Raipur he had behaved rottenly. And worse, he had disgraced himself. Himself, not me. I pointed out some of his revolting personal habits and his self-centred ways. I told him stinginess was one of the world's most unattractive traits. And stinginess wasn't about giving generous gifts. It was much more than that. He was stingy with his time, attention and emotions. A man who pays no attention before, during and after sex to anything but the spurt of his sperm, often on a lady's unsuspecting face, making her recoil and blink, is a man with no refinement.

I also added a few genuine and tender sentences and told him how I had stopped enjoying kachoris and samosas after he left me. It was okay to say this, because I felt no anger, no bitterness. I felt a little sorry for him, because he was so unaware and caught up in his own limited world. Whereas I was free like those parrots on the neem tree. I had wings and I felt beautiful when I looked at myself in the mirror. The sky was mine. And there was no limit to my imagination as I flew around inside my head, without feeling scared. Ruchir from Raipur was trapped. I wasn't.

My letter was not an accusation. It was to let him know I was okay. And I still had feelings for him. If he ever felt like talking to me, he should not hesitate thinking I'd be furious. He thought he was rejecting me. But I didn't feel rejected! I felt myself. Nobody could change that feeling. There were so many things I wanted to write, but then I thought I should be considerate. All of this emotional offloading would have been too much for him to handle. He didn't know, poor man, that I had understood him. Accepted him. That was still true. I even understood why he could no longer marry me—he was ashamed of himself. Not me. After five pages, I stopped. I could have kept writing. But even parrots get tired after a while. I wanted to find a high branch on that beautiful tree and sit there staring at the world, with a gentle breeze to sway me. I didn't want a nest. Nor did I want the company of other parrots.

My desire was to fly off to the next tree. Not neem. But a tree laden with semi-ripe fruit. I stared at the marble bird bath in the garden downstairs. I wanted to splash around in its warm waters, flap my feathers, shake my tail, sharpen my claws and beak, let out a lusty squawk and fly off. Ruchir from Raipur would have shared many adventures in life with me, had we married. He would have become a parrot himself after a few years. We would both have flown together, here and there ... and eventually he would have loved me. And not my hymen.

~

The man whose wife I became (goodness!), turned out to be an okay sort of a chap. When we were left alone by our family members, to take a short stroll in the garden of the Jamshedpur bungalow, the first thing I said to him in a rush was, 'Look look look … I have to tell you … I am not a virgin. I mean … I was once a virgin … that is … till recently … Then I was not a virgin. But now, I am a virgin again … you know?'

He creased his brows and said in a genuinely perplexed voice, 'No, I don't know! I am trying to figure it out. You mind repeating it all over again?' His eyes were puppy eyes … big and sad and brown, his voice was soft, his shirt was also soft. I had touched it to feel his back muscles properly. His hair was thick and slicked back with oil, I'm not sure if he used mustard or sesame. Babuji preferred sesame. I liked his knuckles. They had character. I wanted him to show his feet, because I liked men who cared about their toe nails. A man who neglects his feet is generally sloppy about other things too.

Oh yes … I liked his name. Abudaya had a nice ring to it. Solid. So, I was hoping he'd like me and we'd get married soon. But I had to be frank with him first. So, when he didn't understand my virgin story, I took him near the edge of a tiny pond, next to the gazebo in the garden. I was looking for a muddy patch and a twig. I asked him to go find a twig while I searched for mud. He didn't protest, and was soon back with a sturdy twig from the ficus hedge. I told him to crouch next to me, as I cleared a small mud patch … I drew it all out in simple diagrams, the kind you find in children's science textbooks. Simple sketches, which explained everything step by step.

He looked thoughtfully at my diagrams without laughing or getting impatient. At that moment I turned to him and announced, 'Squirrel!' He looked up and asked, 'Where?' I poked him near his heart and said, 'Here!' He stared at me and smiled. I think he understood. I looked at my diagrams, picked up the twig and scratched them out. 'I will call you Squirrel forever, okay? Even after we get married. You are my Squirrel.'

He held out his hand and I placed mine in it. He looked into my eyes and said, 'Promise?' So, it was final, then. We strolled back to the waiting families. They had probably guessed it was a 'yes' from the boy's side. My response would have been of no consequence.

When we reached them seated on the lawns playing 'statue', I burst out laughing and announced, 'Meet my Squirrel. We are now engaged.' The families clapped and Buaji came towards us bearing a silver salver with bundi laddoos on it. And a velvet jewellery box. I wondered what would have happened to the laddoos had Squirrel rejected me. Would the servants and durwans have eaten them?

I hugged Buaji as Ma looked on, a small smile playing on her lips. She held up her right hand and I noticed she had crossed her delicate fingers. 'Good luck, sweetie,' she mouthed and excused herself.

I whispered into Buaji's left ear as I snuggled into her

ample, warm and rhythmically heaving bosom, 'I told Squirrel everything! I drew diagrams when he didn't get it ... you know, that virgin thing. I don't think he cared.'

Buaji's tight smile, tightened just a little bit more, 'That's what you think, Srilaa ... that's what you think. Wait! You will find out some day. All men care, take it from me. But for now, there's a lot of work to be done. Shaadi hai!'

~

My days as a virgin who was not a virgin were numbered. I found that most exciting! I couldn't wait to have sex with Squirrel. It was decided by Buaji that we would only meet two days before the wedding. She wasn't taking any chances, and I was enjoying the anticipation. I visualised a naked Squirrel and fantasised about him frequently. I knew he would be very different from Ruchir from Raipur. But was not sure how different and in what way.

Buaji used to repeat, 'All men are the same' every time I talked to her about Squirrel. And I would wonder how she could say that. Men are not the same at all. Babuji was Babuji, right? And Squirrel was unknown to me.

We were allowed to speak over the phone, but Buaji was always present. 'Unsupervised calls at this stage can lead to trouble. The less you reveal to Abhudaya about yourself, the better for you. He will dream about you till your wedding night ... that is the real fun, Srilaa. Men should never know too much about a woman. You can keep his interest alive only if you hold back. Once you give your body ... what is left to give?'

What a funny thing to say, I used to think. As if there is nothing else to me ... was I just breasts and skin and armpits and buttocks and thighs and hair and lips and vagina? Would Squirrel stop loving me once he went inside? I managed to ask him that during a phone call.

Buaji had stepped into the other room to fetch a bowl of pistachios. 'Squirrel ... answer quickly—once you fuck me will you stop loving me? That's what Buaji keeps telling me. Say "No"! Or, I won't marry you.' I heard Squirrel laugh before he said solemnly, 'Your diagrams were very interesting. We have so much to talk about, Srilaaji ...'

I screeched, 'What did you just call me?' He repeated slowly and carefully, 'Srilaaji. You will always be Srilaaji to me. Always.'

PART TWO

WIFE

My 'shaadi' was like any other Marwari shaadi—big and showy. I think Buaji had emptied out the tijori and arranged all the sets across my body, while my wrists were weighed down with ten bangles, maybe twenty, on each. The earrings, which belonged to Babuji's mother but had been rejected by Ma for not 'being her style', were forced on me. They were not my style, either. But Buaji said, 'This is our parampara.' What nonsense! What sort of a parampara was this?

My earlobes were bleeding with the jhumkas almost tearing them. But the family elders had to be impressed, 'Our bahu is very traditional ... she touches our feet ... not like these modern girls who say "Hi-bye", wear pant-shirt and leave the house.'

Oh God! Buaji must have lied and lied and lied about all my virtues. Wait till my in-laws found out. I had barely a few seconds to look at Squirrel through all this madness. My eyes were watering from the gigantic hawan's smoke. I glanced at him through the heavy layers of double ghunghats—really, this was Buaji taking things a bit too far to prove how traditional I was. Double ghungats! Squirrel was looking at me, too, and smiling sweetly. He looked uncomfortable and comical in his sherwani and that lop-sided turban with pearls and emeralds and what not. He was wearing three strands of perfectly graded Basra pearls around his neck. I knew they belonged to his grandfather, and were Basra, because Buaji had told me in hushed tones, hoping to further impress me about the grandeur that awaited me in my new life as a Marwari Bahu.

'The servants will address you as Bhabhiji,' she said. I giggled, 'Why not as Madamji? Nobody calls Ma "Bhabhiji".'

Buaji snapped, 'You are not your mother. She is ... she is ... how do I put it ... different.' I pulled a face and said, 'I also want to be different. I want to be like Ma.'

Buaji lost a little colour, looked away and ordered fresh nimbu paani. 'Please remove any such idea from your head, Srilaa. For your own sake.' That closed the Ma topic permanently.

The wedding ceremonies went on and on. By the time I was escorted up to the bridal chamber by a bunch of silly, overdressed, noisy women (Squirrel's cousins), I wanted to gulp down a large glass of whiskey. Neat. And maybe, smoke a few cigarettes. I looked at the gigantic four poster bed which was bedecked with flowers—red and pink roses, chamelis, orange and yellow marigolds, purple orchids, bright red anthuriums ... and my first thought was, 'Don't these people have better sense than to combine so many different flowers and colours?'

The women were singing wedding songs and were out of tune most of the time. I had spotted Ma, but had not spoken to her. Babuji was with the menfolk, and looking wonderful in a white dhoti, long coat and Marwari pugdi. He was not wearing pearls. But his Golconda diamond buttons caught the light of the leaping flames from the hawan and created many brilliant galaxies. He seemed happy. It was difficult to tell with Babuji. Ma did come to the mandap to bless me during the kanyadan rituals. She looked distracted and in a daze. But glorious, nevertheless. She was wearing a delicate gold tissue saree and hardly any jewellery, except for a magnificent ruby brooch holding up her saree pallu on the left shoulder. And I know she said some sweet things, but I couldn't hear above the din of the punditji's chanting.

'Our family prefers Vedic rituals,' Buaji was told and she had nodded, 'Same as ours.' Now that the Vedic rituals were over, I wanted to lie naked with Squirrel—my brand new husband—and fuck crazily till the bulbuls arrived for their morning bird seeds.

By the time he was done with his part of the absurd rituals, the bulbuls were already chirping outside the large bay windows of our marital chamber. The mixed fragrances from all those unmatched flowers were making me nauseous. I had torn the clothes off myself, rejecting the offers of maids sent to help me undress.

The elaborate lehenga was thrown on the carpet, along with the uncomfortable zari sandals, backless choli, the 'double ghunghat', and my special panties from London (Buaji had taken a lot of trouble to select and order my lingerie).

I had fallen asleep waiting for Squirrel, but woke up when I heard a thud. The lights were off, and I was startled. Where had the noise come from? I wondered, while groping for the switch of the bedside lamp. I was unfamiliar with the switches in my new room and it took me a while to find the right one. When the light came on I saw a body sprawled on the floor near the heavy sheesham door with the shiny brass handle—it was Squirrel!

He was lying face down on the carpet, completely entangled in my lehenga, with one of my sandals on his shoulders. The fall had displaced his turban which was now balanced at a crazy angle on his head. I rushed to him ... I was naked, but for the lace London panties. 'Squirrel! What happened?' I cried. He threw off my lehenga from his body, pushed away the turban, sat on his haunches and smiled broadly (my double ghunghats were still around him), 'Relax, Srilaaji ... let me look at you. Let me look at my wife!'

I burst out laughing, 'Idiot! What ... look at you ... look at you ... look at you. You can look later, aaram se. Stop wasting time, Squirrel! Get up ... get inside me! Chalo, chalo! Jaldi karo!'

And that was my wedding night. My first night as a wife!

What was Squirrel like as a lover? Well, at that point I had only known one other man—Ruchir from Raipur. Ruchir was a fast food delivery fellow. Always in a hurry to leave. Squirrel was more like a thali served in an Udupi place—he wanted to taste everything and then ask for more. No leftovers! Thali licked clean. Full paisa vasool.

'Make the most of it,' he said, as he took his time to enter me. An hour of leisurely feasting later, there was just enough space left for roasted saunf. That was when I started keeping a glass jar filled with freshly roasted saunf by my bedside. It became my trademark over the years. 'Srilaaji's saunf!' It also became our code for love-making. 'Srilaaji ... hope you have roasted some saunf today ...' Squirrel would say at the dining table, a sly, sideways look thrown in my direction. I would reply, 'There is always a lot of saunf kept especially for you to enjoy.'

Our private joke became stale after a while. Like our sex. Nothing new was tried. Even though I kept suggesting little tricks. Nothing dirty or disgusting. Just new areas to savour with our tongues. Squirrel would get put off and sulk like a kid. 'I only like doing that!' he'd say before turning away listlessly.

Soon, our daily saunf sessions, became weekly, then monthly, then bi-monthly ... but by then I had discovered my own body and what to do with it. Of course, I missed a man's touch and I definitely missed

Squirrel's organ, which was pretty impressive, if a little crooked. But the effort involved to achieve an orgasm was too much. And I knew the patterns on the ceiling so intimately, as I stared at them while Squirrel thrust and heaved and panted, I wanted to hire a ladder and paint over those geometrical designs. Life in that vast home was pretty empty ... so empty, I even considered taking piano lessons. I had started to understand Ma. I didn't want to become my mother. Trapped and frightened. A fragile, little bird afraid to chirp too much.

~

Moving to Bombay was not as easy or glamorous as I had imagined. 'Marwari bahus are treated like Maharanis,' I was repeatedly told by Squirrel's bossy Chaachiji. Anushreedevi ran the sprawling home—one of the few mansions left in South Bombay. I think she liked me, or rather saw a younger version of her own self in me. Well ... she was also fair complexioned. Fairer than Squirrel's mother, who was married off to brother number two, which made her a notch lower down in the family hierarchy than Chaachiji. She was also ten shades darker than her sister-in-law, and had a flatter nose, with prominent nostrils. God knows why she drew more attention to those cavernous nostrils by wearing a chickpea-sized diamond nose pin.

Anushreedevi was technically second-in-command

to Squirrel's paternal grandmother—the lady in the wheel chair. 'Badi Mummy', as she was addressed by all (staff included), was reduced to playing a titular role after her stroke. Nobody understood a word of what she mumbled, except her uniformed nurses from the nearby Breach Candy Hospital. Since the nurses quit frequently, unable to keep up with Badi Mummy's constant and unreasonable demands, it was all the more difficult to figure out what she wanted, but everyone knew she wanted something or the other non-stop.

Anushreedevi indulged her up to a point, especially in the presence of her three sons, but I used to hear her mumble 'bloody bitch' under her breath after she had smiled broadly and said, 'Haanji, Badi Mummy ... I will see to it that the pineapple is properly cut next time.' Fruit cutting was a major job for the ladies of the house. Servants would ceremoniously present trays of fruit for their inspection every morning. Anushreedevi would take her time to pick up each fruit, check for ripeness, and then issue orders. 'No cutting apples today. Only sitaphal and pears for nashta. Pack oranges and grapes—the green Nashik ones—for the Sethlog's dabbas.'

Once the fruit ritual was solemnly concluded, and the trays taken back to the pantry, Anushreedevi would summon her 'lady-in-waiting', the mighty Sarla, to plan her wardrobe for the day. Sarla's sole job was to manage Anushreedevi's multiple cupboards and never mix up the saree petticoats. Sarla knew every blouse, caftan, bra and underwear in those cupboards—which garment was meant to be hand-washed at home, which, sent to the laundry, which to be ironed by the istriwala down the slope, and which by Shankar, the in-house istri man. Sarla also knew every pricey shawl stored in a special wicker basket, which sat in Anushreedevi's airy, well-lit dressing room, with a gigantic Bohemian chandelier on the ceiling. The Persian carpet on the parquet flooring was weathered and worn over the years, but exuded the confident personality of the owner, who wore her vintage with incredible style.

Over time, I became Chaachiji's little chamchi—an acolyte. In a way, she replaced Ma in my otherwise lonely Bombay life. Though, unlike Ma, Anushreedevi was a shrewd, cunning, devious, aggressive master strategist, playing one family member against the other. I admired her gutsiness and the fact that all the men in the household were scared of her, and rarely crossed her path. My own father-in-law stepped back into his room if he spotted her approaching. Initially, I was a bit surprised when I was asked whether I wanted a separate room to myself.

Anushreedevi had winked conspiratorially and said, 'Bitiyarani, it is always better for wives to have their own space in the long run. Just take that lovely room ... keep your things there, and you can always invite your sweet husband to sleep with you in your bed, whenever you are in the mood. Understand? Men also need their space, and in any case, sleeping together every day is so boring

… you will soon get tired. Better to start a marriage with different bedrooms. That corner room may be grabbed by someone else if you don't claim it right away.' It turned out to be excellent advice!

Squirrel and I had a set pattern for our co-habitation—he kept a calendar by his bedside, with my menstrual cycle marked on it. Since we didn't want children for at least two years, he made sure we avoided sex during the fertile period.

'Let's have some fun, Srilaaji,' was his not-so-subtle invitation to get intimate. In my enthusiasm, I would order fragrant chamelis by the kilo, or scatter rose petals on the bed, before getting under the sheets. I would also spray Chanel No. 5 in the air, and liberally all over my body. But Squirrel told me it was a waste. 'Srilaaji … don't mind … but I like your special khushboo.' I was flattered and told him I liked his 'khushboo' too. A lot.

He hugged me, 'See? I knew we were the right match under that stupid tree in Jamshedpur when you were making all those dirty drawings. Now, just think what happens when your khushboo and my khushboo mingle and produce a new khushboo! When we have our daughter, we will name her Khushboo.' I agreed and we both laughed a lot at the thought of raising Khushboo. Instead, I produced a son. That too, within the first year of our marriage. We named him Kushal. Kushal Khaitan … oh … my new surname. I liked it! Srilaa Khaitan, mother of Kushal Khaitan, wife of Squirrel Khaitan.

When I discovered I was pregnant, I was most upset and blamed Squirrel for not wearing a condom. He soothed me by saying, 'But Srilaaji, to become one in our togetherness, we cannot have some other skin in between.' It was too late to protest and even though I was least prepared to become a mother, there I was, waddling around the house, and getting fed every hour by my overjoyed mother-in-law. Oh yes, she, the darker one, came from a very prominent Kanpur clan, and it was believed, she brought such an impressive dowry, nobody talked about her complexion. 'She shut up all the mouths with the pearls and rubies, gold and silver ... suitcases of cash,' Anushreedevi sniggered, adding, 'Me? I only brought my gori chamdi!' What she said so crudely, was an obsession in the family. Women were placed in only two boxes—fair and dark. I asked Squirrel about it, 'Did you marry me only because I was fair complexioned?'

He looked genuinely puzzled before exclaiming, 'Srilaaji ... it is true. Of course! Had you been less fair, I would have waited to find another girl.' I lunged for his balls.

He stepped back nimbly and said, 'Srilaaji, it is time for some saunf.' Shameless fellow. After we had sumptuous and entirely satisfying sex, he said, 'I have a small request—don't mind, okay? Next time the tailor comes home, please tell him to make front openingwala saree blouse.' I laughed ... and asked why. 'It's easy that way ... !'

'Easy?'

Squirrel changed the subject, pinched my nipple and said, 'You ask unnecessary questions. Be patient. You will soon understand ...'

There were very many things I had to understand very quickly. It was a strange set-up, this Khaitan House. And I was not sure where I fitted in. Squirrel was 'given' a car for his use. He didn't own it. But had to pay for the petrol from his personal account. I was allowed to use his car when he wasn't using it. But I had to put in a request with the man in a steel grey safari suit. He was simply addressed as 'Shriji'. He called the men in the family either 'Maalik' or 'Sarkar', and 'Babuji', which was the more traditional form of address in Marwari business families, and spoke to them with his eyes shut, head bowed and the right hand placed over his heart. He was a burly chap and I suspect the Maaliks used him to keep an eye on Anushreedevi's adventures.

Shriji controlled the movement of all the cars and the drivers were terrified of him. Even the durwans behaved like he was the boss. I had never seen him smile. Or take a day off. He was just there! I think all the drivers were his carefully screened nominees who spied on all of us and gave him a daily briefing. He, in turn, passed on relevant, well-timed information to the personal secretaries who worked for the Khaitan men.

No female secretaries were considered, as Squirrel explained solemnly. 'Srilaaji ... don't mind but generally we believe it is better to employ men. Women create too many problems—they want to grab our money, break up our marriages, reveal our secrets. Too much tension!' So I asked him if I could have my own car and driver someday, since I felt claustrophobic, like I was being constantly watched.

Squirrel laughed and agreed with me whole heartedly, 'Yes. You are being watched. All the women in the family are watched. It is for your own safety.' I immediately made a mental note to find ways to trick Shriji. I succeeded! I declared myself a 'social worker' and told Shriji I needed the car every day to feed orphans in different localities of Bombay. Ma's social work 'alibi' was a very useful tip.

Shriji looked most impressed. 'Bhabhiji, you are very noble. No problem, no problem. A car will always be there for you. Cannot let gareeb children starve. It is a maha paap.' I wanted to become a maha paapi myself! But that would take time. At that moment I was busy finding my feet in a Marwari household where nobody trusted anybody, and everybody spoke in riddles. I could never figure out what was being said at the dining table. They spoke in a dialect I was not familiar with. The elders said the servants were listening. I felt it was okay if they were listening.

Till Squirrel told me they could be spies planted by rival business families, 'Srilaaji, we have so many secrets to guard. Business secrets, personal secrets. It is not good to trust anybody. And servants are the worst traitors.

Servants and hajaams. When that man comes to shave me every morning, it is better not to say anything in his presence, okay?'

Charity work saved me. I mean, initially I got into it only to get out of the house. I told Squirrel I was keen on doing social service. He replied, 'It is a good thing. Do it from Khaitan House. We have many children of the servants and drivers. You can teach them English. Your English is good, very good. Convent English.'

I thanked him and said I had a different plan. I had found an NGO working out of a small office on Worli Sea Face. I liked the team and ... and ... most of the ladies were also Marwari ... from good families.

Squirrel looked very worried. 'I am not sure Badi Mummy will approve. Or my mummy. Or anybody.'

So I left the armchair I was comfortably seated on and went and sat on Squirrel's lap. 'Look ... I got that blouse stitched ... the one with front buttons ... see?' And I pulled down my saree pallu from the left shoulder and let it trail on the carpet. The deep, scooped neckline of my blouse revealed a lot of breast. Squirrel's eyes nearly popped out of their sockets as he started blabbering incoherently, his fingers working overtime to undo the buttons.

Finally, he gave up and just dug in frantically, like he was in search of a gold nugget. Well ... he found it! The minute his forefinger and thumb located my nipple, he groaned, 'Srilaaji ... Srilaaji ... Oh, Srilaaji ... you don't know what is happening to me ...'

I placed my hand on his crotch and smiled, 'Of course, I know! So glad you liked my front buttons ... convenient and easy. No wasting precious time.'

He sighed, 'Yes, time is precious ... very precious. Next time, let's try in the backseat of the car. Don't worry ... not during the day, Srilaaji ... but we can go for a drive to Juhu at night ... and then at Worli Sea Face ... phataphat ... ?'

After that, we stopped wasting precious time. And I started working for the NGO. Oh yes, Squirrel dipped into his precious personal account and bought me a car. A small one. But at least I didn't have to ask Shriji's permission before stepping out anymore. The driver was also paid for by Squirrel, after a round of arguments and discussions with the family elders. I overheard him saying over and over again, 'Why are all of you so worried? I am telling you, she will not do anything! I am standing guarantee for my wife. You catch me if she does any gadbad. I have full faith in her. She is doing good social work by feeding orphans. Those poor children need her or they'll starve.'

Sweet Squirrel. I stitched many more front open blouses, and varied the necklines. Some were deep V-necks, some scooped, some had stitched in bra cups which freed up my breasts even more. I had a lot of fun designing these blouses, and my Gujarati tailor from Girgaum used to giggle and stare pointedly at my breasts when he came home for fittings. I am sure he knew. Once he made a stray comment and said, 'Many newly married ladies switch from back opening to front opening. It makes breast feeding easy.' I was about to say, 'But I don't have a baby!' I bit my lip and kept quiet. Squirrel was my baby. He had not been weaned. He knew how to latch and suck. He would always remain my baby.

My mother-in-law was a good teacher. I felt comfortable talking to her. Even about Squirrel and his strange habits. 'Was he like this when he was a small boy?' I asked after Squirrel had thrown a fit about his night clothes not being ironed properly by his designated man servant. I had laughed and said, 'But you are wearing this night suit to bed! Nobody will see those creases.' Squirrel had looked pained and replied, 'Srilaaji ... you won't understand. You are not a man. Our testicles are very sensitive. If the wrong crease of the pajama gets trapped between the testicles and the inner thigh, proper sleep cannot happen.'

Actually, I did understand. I told Squirrel to undress and get into the wrongly creased pajamas so that I could instruct the man servant how to get it right. He did so obediently and lay on his side, with the pajama crease rubbing against his right testicle. 'See?' It is a major problem, Srilaaji.' There were other 'male problems' he patiently explained to me. Some had to do with digestion. Others with hairy navels. Still others with buttocks which were not perfectly spherical and equal. His mother was familiar with all these problems and not in the least bit embarrassed discussing them with a daughter-in-law.

She told me over til ka laddoos (it was Sankranti, and the laddoos were still hot after the jaggery syrup had congealed in the palms of the Maharaj and his kitchen staff as they shaped the mixture into tiny, tightly packed balls) that men have many problems. It is up to women which problems to pay attention to and which to ignore. 'Men can be very childish. It is okay. Treat your husband like a child when he is in that mood. Men also forget. Women remember everything. That is our advantage and also our biggest disadvantage. We should also forget what does not suit us and pretend we are feeling fine, like most men do. Woh English word kya hai? Amnesia! Men suffer from selective amnesia. Your husband also masturbates in his sleep. He used to shake the bed so violently when he was just seven or eight years old. I would wake up and shake him. It's an old habit. Ignore it. Because it is harmless. Better he touched himself than other women. Or men.'

I didn't realise then that she was trying to tell me something important about Squirrel. Years later, her words came back to me, when Squirrel fell in love with Soumitro—a junior executive in a steel company. It took me time to figure it out. But I was not at all angry. I loved Squirrel the way he was—an innocent, trusting explorer. If Soumitro made him happy, it made me happy. We never discussed Soumitro. I felt it was better that way. And I cuddled Squirrel with the same amount of love as the first time we spent the night together after our wedding. Even with Soumitro in his life, Squirrel continued to make love to me, with as much tenderness and affection as before. We were 'made for each other', as the cigarette slogan declared. And I liked my life as his wife and the bahu of the parivar. I was bored for sure. But not unhappy-unhappy.

It was when Squirrel and I were driving to the Sea Lounge to enjoy a Viennoise—his favourite ice cream—that I suggested a holiday in Bangkok. For fun. Not shopping.

He took a scoop of the ice cream in a spoon and held it to my mouth, 'Lick!' he said. So I licked. Squirrel stared out at the waves hitting the parapet around the Gateway of India.

'Let me ask Soumitro,' he said softly but firmly.

'Ask him what? Permission to take your wife for a holiday?' I commented, my voice a little raised.

Squirrel stared some more at the waves. 'Not like that. Not permission, as such ... but I don't want to hurt his feelings.' It took me a few seconds to take that in.

I snapped, 'His feelings! What about my feelings?' We were seated near the bay windows and facing each other.

Squirrel reached over and held my hand, 'Srilaaji ... calm down. Soumitro is my special friend. You are my wife. Two different categories. What's the issue? I am sure he won't say "no". He is not like that.'

'Not like what? Like me? Who is he to say yes or no? Is it too much to expect a husband to take his wife for a holiday? Who is being unreasonable—you or me?'

'Srilaaji ... please excuse me. But I need to talk to Soumitro before we plan the trip. Okay?' He held up another scoop of Viennoise for me to lick. This time, I not just licked it but ate up the entire portion. Squirrel looked hurt. His anguish made me feel sorry for him. I kicked off my sandals, and tickled his calves with my bared toes.

Squirrel giggled and protested, 'Stop it, Srilaaji ... people are staring!' So I started giggling, too. Soon both of us were giggling and throwing napkins at one another. It was hard to stay angry with Squirrel.

On the drive back, I gazed at the lights stringing the famous Queen's Necklace. Bombay was a seductress. I was helpless. I turned to Squirrel and purred, 'I have a good solution to the Bangkok problem. Let's invite Soumitro to Bangkok. That way you'll be happy, and I will get to roam around Bangkok on a motorcycle.'

Squirrel reacted to 'motor cycle' as I had expected him to. 'Srilaaji, you never told me you rode bikes?'

I smiled, 'I have not told you many things, Squirrel, because you have never asked! Had you asked, "Srilaaji ... do you ride motorcycles?" when we met in Jamshedpur, I would have told you the truth—I don't.'

Squirrel was perplexed, 'Then?'

I laughed, 'I have heard there are motorcycle taxis in Bangkok. They are cheaper and quicker than regular taxis. I will prefer those to a hired limousine. You and Soumitro use the car. I will jump on a bike? Okay?'

And that settled it. Soumitro became an intimate part of our married life and travelled everywhere with us. In a way, it worked out very well. I was left alone to do what I wanted, see what I wanted, go where I wanted to. Squirrel and Soumitro would be so wrapped up in their world, they barely noticed. It was all rather sweet and touching. They'd book spa treatments and massages together. Saunas and steam sessions became a part of the daily routine. The three of us would plan dinners together and let Soumitro do the ordering (he was a gourmet cook and a connoisseur of all things fine and wonderful, including wine). Through Soumitro, Squirrel and I made several discoveries, not just those involving food, but also films, music and fashion.

Soumitro became my style guide and shopping companion, unfailingly picking colours, cuts and styles that suited my body type (pear-shaped). He advised me to buy the right brassieres for different outfits. Lingerie shopping was so much fun with Soumitro carefully picking out the appropriate bra and correcting my posture. 'You slouch too much, Mrs Khaitan,' he said to me as we went through rows of delicious lingerie at a fancy store.

'Do I really?' I asked, immediately straightening my shoulders.

'It is because your shoulders are small and delicate, Mrs Khaitan, and your cup size is D. There is an imbalance ... you have to keep your neck high and chest out. Or else, your bosom will sag before you turn thirty. Then, by the time you turn fifty, there will be a major problem, Mrs Khaitan.' Oh dear. This man knew everything.

He even kept track of my menstrual cycles, along with Squirrel and knew it was that time of the month by merely observing me. And yes, I was always 'Mrs Khaitan' to him. After all, he was a junior executive—not our equal. Soumitro knew his place.

Squirrel addressed him as 'Shomu' when they were alone, and stuck to Soumitro in company. I am not sure what they called each other in bed. But that was their business. I never asked. Squirrel did not get jealous. I found that odd. I tried flirting with Soumitro in Squirrel's presence once or twice, but it was no fun. I danced tantalisingly to an old Helen number, swaying my hips and shaking my breasts. The two of them looked bored and mildly irritated, waiting for me to stop acting silly. 'Srilaaji ... drink?' Squirrel asked waving a tumbler of whiskey in my face. Both of them had started meeting every evening for a round of drinks on the balcony. Drinks and fried snacks—I had taught the Maharaj how to make crisp vegetable spring rolls. Eight pieces—four each. Squirrel liked to sprinkle kasundi on his, while Soumitro preferred tomato ketchup. All three of us discovered Thai cuisine when we went to Bangkok. Whiskey and Pad Thai went well together.

It was during that first trip to Bangkok that someone tried to pick me up. I was waiting near the elevators when a stylishly dressed, statuesque woman in very high heels walked up to me and said, 'Are you looking for company?' Somewhat startled and quite at a loose end, I replied, 'Yes. Sure.'

The person smiled and slid into the elevator with me. I was inexperienced enough at the time to think we would have room service deliver coffee, perhaps cheese sandwiches and pastries, chat a little, and say 'bye bye'. Squirrel and Soumitra had booked a ninety-minute Thai massage at the spa, and I had nothing better to do. Our suite was interconnected to Soumitro's room, and the whole thing had worked out quite smoothly—sleeping arrangements, bathroom use and all that.

When I shut the door of the suite behind me, I saw the statuesque person kick off those heels, pull off the elaborate wig, and start unbuttoning the shirt dress. 'Wait ... Hey you! What are you doing?' I screamed.

The person in front of me ignored my screams and calmly stripped down to a red lace bra and ... and ... a red G-string. 'Surprise!' came a throaty growl and off snapped the G-string, revealing an impressive, erect penis. Frankly, I felt more confused than horrified. I didn't like being ambushed.

'I am here to please you ... my name is Lia Lilly,' he said, holding out his hand. Yes, the wrist belonged to a man, the hands had prominent veins, and up close, I could see a huge Adam's apple bobbing up and down each time he swallowed. I started to stutter, 'I'm not sure

... I am scared ... please go away ... my husband will be back any minute ... here, take my bag, help yourself ... open my wallet ... take the money, but please leave.'

Lia Lilly sneered, 'Scared pussy. Okay. Give me the money. But I think you should try me first. Then you could recommend me to other rich Indian ladies. I am gooooooood.' Lia Lilly picked up his penis and waved it near my face, 'See? Big and strong. Better than your husband's ... try ... just try. No disease. I'll be quick. Five minutes—and finished. Boom. Over.' It took three.

Not five.

I took down Lia Lilly's number on a paper napkin. If Squirrel or Soumitro asked me whose number it was, I would say the hair dresser's. Over time, Lia Lilly and I became friends. I would carry gifts from India for Lia Lilly. Mainly cosmetics and perfumes. Food, as well. With Lia Lilly I discovered a Bangkok that Squirrel would never have let me enjoy. It was a simple, gentle Bangkok, far from the tourist attractions and luxury malls. Far from sleazy Pat Pong and filthy massage parlours. I felt comfortable in Lia Lilly's world. And his friends accepted me as 'That rich lady from India with very big breasts'.

Breasts were an obsession in Lia Lilly's close-knit community. Silicone implants didn't come cheap. Lia Lilly used to keep fondling my breasts, treating them like wondrous objects. And I liked his penis. It's angle and girth. 'My beautiful dick has made me popular and famous.' Lia Lilly would say with child-like pride.

As a birthday treat, I offered to replace Lia Lilly's implants. He started to cry. 'Nobody has done so much for me ... nobody. You are an angel.' I even thought of introducing him to Squirrel. Then I felt bad about betraying Soumitro. I think they were faithful to each other. Though I can't be too sure. I used to catch Soumitro eyeing other men, even during official events and formal functions. My own feelings were pretty mixed. Sometimes I felt left out when the two of them were so totally engrossed in one another. At other times, I felt like sleeping with Soumitro, just to find out what Squirrel experienced during their lovemaking. Of course, I knew it would be entirely different with me. Even so.

It was Soumitro who offered me a cigarette—555 it was officially called. Squirrel had stepped out for an errand and the two of us were gazing at the gulmohur tree in full bloom across the road. It was my favourite tree. It reminded me of Chumkididi. I missed her in a strange way. Ma hardly ever called, and when she did, the conversation was limited to, 'Sweetie, I do hope you have found a good manicurist in your city. Nails are very important.' So, when Soumitro held out a pack and raised his left eyebrow quizzically, I wordlessly took out a cigarette and waited for him to light it.

He reached into his trouser pocket and took out a silver lighter. I noticed it was a sleek Cartier and inscribed with his initials. 'Gift?' I asked. Soumitro nodded, 'From him.' Soumitro never uttered Squirrel's name. I took a long drag and blew out a plume of smoke. I didn't cough. It wasn't my first ciggie. The smoke felt so good. Soumitro smiled and we continued to stare at the Gulmohur, lost in our respective worlds.

When Squirrel returned, he stared at the ash tray and glared at Soumitro. 'So many?' Soumitro looked slightly sheepish as he said, 'Mrs Khaitan tried one or two ...' Squirrel remained silent for a moment before smiling broadly, 'I seeeeeeee ... welcome to the club.' That was that. Now their bad habit had become mine. We were equal.

Making friends in Bombay was not easy. I soon discovered it wasn't worth the effort. I had very little in common with other Marwari wives. And I was only exposed to these ladies by Squirrel's family. I felt very disconnected listening to their cackling conversations about mother-in-law problems and how difficult it was to manage with the paltry 'house money' given to them by their miserly husbands.

'I try and try and try ... but how much can I cheat on daily sabzi and grocery accounts? He counts the number of potatoes in every kilo and keeps a track of who eats how much ghee.' It was either that track or endless bitching about which woman stole her friend's Maharaj. Imagine. Maharaj. Not husband. It was generally agreed that a good Maharaj was far more valuable than a fantastic husband. One could always get another fantastic husband ... but never a great Maharaj capable of making dal batti that could send guests into a food coma with its texture and taste.

Then there was jewellery talk. Who had flaunted what at the Udaipur wedding ... and was it asli or fake stuff?

'We wear costume jewellery these days ... security issues. Actually, our family jeweller gets his karigars to make two sets always—one with real gold and diamonds, the other, an exact replica in gold plated silver with imitation stones. Better to be safe.' I had made the mistake of asking what the ladies did with the genuine pieces if they didn't wear them.

They looked at me pityingly and said, 'Tijori. We all have large tijoris to store our jewellery.'

I persisted, 'It is never to be worn? What's the point of having it?'

One lady looking particularly exasperated, explained tersely, 'Arrey baba ... but we know it is there, na? We know how much it costs. Bas! That is enough.'

Sarees and lehengas were discussed with so much enthusiasm and excitement, I imagined some of the women experiencing an orgasm as they sighed and squealed about the patola they had booked or the leheriya they had acquired. Once or twice, I tried to talk about other things, but nobody was interested. They'd smile, roll their eyes and say, 'You are from Calcutta, na? Your life is very different ... that's why.' That's why—what?

I was being the 'goodwife'—an obedient, duty-conscious Marwari bahu who may have had plenty of money to spend, but was always trying to impress her in-laws by showing how frugal she was when it came to daily kharcha. I had heard Marwari bahus from our posh neighbourhood had their favourite phoolwalas at Prarthana Samaj—a colourful, crowded area near the famed Royal Opera House, where one pavement was reserved for flower sellers who created the most beautiful gajras and fragrant garlands for deities in our home temples.

These specialised phoolwalas preferred to make Bhagwan ka garlands for women like me, who drove up in good cars, rolled down the window and said, 'Ufff ... no fresh mogra kalis today? This is terrible. My Sri Krishna will be so upset. Okay ... give me two garlands anyway, but at half price since the flowers are stale.'

It was during these excursions that I noticed bahus in other cars behaving in an odd way. While the drivers were busy paying the phoolwala, they would be hastily undressing in the backseat of their sedans! Not undressing completely of course but removing their sarees and half-ghunghats to reveal sexy, western-style tops in place of traditional cholis. Once the saree was off, and neatly folded, one could spot tight blue jeans instead of the expected saree petticoat in matching colours. The bahus were off to meet their boyfriends!

I wondered how they managed to get back into their sarees before heading home. Soon, a giggling young thing I befriended near 'my' phoolwala, told me, 'Six seconds!'

I asked, 'Six seconds for what?' She answered, 'I can pull off and re-drape my saree in six seconds! Try it at home—it's easy once you practice how to manage the pleats.'

I never managed! I always got caught. The six-second saree defeated my best romance plans!

Srilaaji's Fantasy

Mrs Binani is in the bathroom undressing slowly. Her pendulous breasts sway back and forth as she bends over to step out of her beige underwear. Her hips are huge and dimpled. Her thighs, deeply pitted with bags of cellulite hanging like mini-pouches on either side. Her pubic hair is thick and unruly, with bunches growing erratically and extending onto her inner thighs. She squats on a low stool and pours water over her head, temporarily shutting her eyes. Suddenly, the bathroom door opens, and two young maids walk in with a male servant. All three of them take turns to bathe Mrs Binani, while she continues to keep her eyes shut. Once they are done bathing her, they leave silently, and her favourite dog joins her. Mrs Binani opens her eyes and starts petting him lovingly. Rocky begins to lick Mrs Binani's toes, with their brightly painted toenails. She coos and pats Rocky some more. Rocky is clearly excited and happy. He continues to lick his mistress all over her body, and places his front legs on her shoulders ... Mrs Binani closes her eyes again. And surrenders to Rocky.

The ladies of Bombay were right. My life was very different from theirs. What they were wrong about was that they imagined I wanted to be like them. No, I didn't! And I consoled myself thinking had Squirrel wanted to marry one of them, he could have done so easily. He was the prized Marwari bachelor they were all eyeing before he said 'yes' to me. His net worth was a topic of animated discussion at Marwari gatherings. His family tree was etched on their minds. His great grandfather had been a leader of the community back then, and his business acumen was still discussed in hushed tones.

How he came to Bombay with nothing in his pocket, no education, no backing. How he started his life in crowded Kalbadevi carrying iron rods for a local merchant. From being a coolie and winning the trust of his employer, he became a supervisor and had five coolies reporting to him. It was said he could beat anybody at numbers and calculations. With some additional money in his pocket he started trading in commodities. Soon, he became a trader with clout. From trading to setting up his own trading company along with a modest manufacturing unit dealing in polyester yarn spindles, he grew his business till one day, eighteen years after his arrival in Bombay, he became the undisputed leader in spindles and other textile machinery. Once he established himself, he launched Khaitan Industries, and after he made a huge killing in the stock market, he decided to focus on philanthropy, letting his four sons carry on with the business. He retired as a lion in the community, feared and respected by all. In fact, so proud were they about their ancestors, an entire wall in the corridor leading to the dining room was covered with garlanded portraits of these pugree-wala men. Did they not have wives? Why wasn't a single woman represented on that wall? I smiled at the thought: one day I would tell Squirrel to hang a sexy portrait of mine in the same corridor.

Squirrel loved to narrate his great grandfather's story, especially to foreign guests at our home. They would listen attentively as Squirrel held forth, pointing reverentially to a life-size oil painting of his forefather, that hung on the wall of the high-ceilinged dining room. This man with such a lineage had chosen me! Not the lady who became Mrs Somani after Squirrel rejected her. Not any of the other 'Bombay girls' with all their pretensions. Squirrel had picked me. Why did he say 'Yes' to my proposal when he had so much choice? The answer was obvious. He wasn't attracted to any of them. Squirrel had fallen for me. Yes, me!

And then, I behaved stupidly and fell for someone else! I should have considered myself very blessed and fortunate. I was repeatedly told how lucky I was to marry into such an illustrious family. I liked Squirrel. It was not as if I was unhappy or anything. By the time I fell for 'that man' (Why identify him? Let him remain 'that man'), I had produced our 'Khusboo'. The second child that is not considered mandatory if the first one is a boy. But

Squirrel and I had decided we would go for a second one, regardless. I knew the loneliness and isolation of being an only child. Besides, Kushal needed a companion, we reasoned, and we were both young and healthy enough to go ahead and have a second.

I went back to Kolkata for Khusboo's delivery. Buaji thought it would be a good idea. And Ma sounded enthusiastic, 'Sweetie ... remember to rub freshly pressed almond oil on your belly. Those awful stretch marks! They show through chiffon, you know, darling?' I was full term and bloated beyond recognition, when I met 'that man' at Mocambo. I was by myself, attacking a baked crab, when a voice from the next table said, 'Are you sure you should be eating crab in your condition?' My mouth was full as I twisted my neck to see who it was offering unsolicited advice.

Hmmmmmmm. I promptly forgot all about the half-eaten crab or that my mouth was full. I declared, 'My God! You are so cute!' And he was! He grinned, 'I get that a lot ... but rarely from pregnant ladies who look like they might pop any moment.'

I patted to a place next to me on the sofa and said, 'Come, come, come. Come and sit with me, you cutie.' And he did.

He swiftly left his table, after picking up his coffee cup, and smoothly slid on to the sofa, sitting daringly close right next to me and laughing, 'Mad woman!'

I shook my head energetically and agreed

wholeheartedly, 'You are right! I am totally mad.' That's how our affair began—over half-eaten baked crab and half-drunk coffee.

He had laughing eyes. And he made me laugh. Squirrel had stopped amusing me a while ago. His smiles, jokes and laughter were reserved for Soumitro. His rages, too. These days, Squirrel would shout and scream like a hysterical woman if Soumitro arrived ten minutes later than agreed. Or didn't show up at all. He would abuse him and say the most awful things. The accusations started to escalate. Squirrel would fly into a jealous rage and throw around names of other attractive young men known to both of them. He'd sniff Soumitro's shirts and demand explanations if the standard fragrance had been swapped for some other.

But his worst rebuke was reserved for occasions when Soumitro went out of town on 'work'. Squirrel would splutter and fume, throw whatever came handy on the floor, and finally end up crying. When Squirrel wept, it broke my heart ... he sobbed like a kid, sniffling and repeating over and over again, 'He doesn't love me ... I know it. I think he is in love with someone else.' I would comfort Squirrel by holding him close to my bosom and rocking him gently till he fell asleep.

He would mumble 'Thank you, Srilaaji ...' And drift off, his breath heavy, his chest heaving rhythmically. Sweet Squirrel. I told him there was just one way to keep Soumitro all to himself. 'Buy him a flat close by. Give him a car and a driver. Look after him generously. Make sure he has enough shopping money and spending money. Give him much more than he expects or dreams about. That way, he will feel ashamed about seeing any other person. Plus, he will feel grateful to you. Upgrades are necessary from time to time. In offices they call it a pay rise. Employees must be incentivised or they stray.'

Squirrel listened gravely and then said, 'Srilaaji ... you are a genius.' My plan didn't work. Soumitro hung around for a few more months, took whatever Squirrel gave him. And vanished. We were told he had landed a well-paid job in Canada, and was planning to marry a local girl of Indian origin in Vancouver.

'That Man' was relaxed and confident and asked nothing of me. I wanted nothing from him either. Well ... we both wanted uncomplicated sex. That much was clearly understood. He was a boxwalla, a tea man. He travelled a lot, and enjoyed his life. He casually mentioned a long-term girlfriend in Delhi, and an ex-wife in Kolkata. They were all close friends and met frequently in either city. What was I to him? God knows. But I knew I was something when we met at the bar of the Oberoi Grand when Khusboo was two months old.

'Are you nursing the baby?' he asked. And my hands flew to my nipples. Yes, my saree had a large milk patch which was growing and growing, even though I still had an hour to go before Khusboo's next feed.

He ordered a dry martini (with three olives—just three), and I stuck to freshly squeezed orange juice. 'Why don't you add some Campari to it? The baby will love the new taste ... start them young, I always say.'

'Shut up! You are such a bad influence,' I responded.

'Aren't you bored of good influences? Goody goody people? Go on, admit it.' Of course, I was! But I didn't know too many people outside my circle. This was a little new to me.

He asked cheekily, 'What if your Marwari friends see you here, having a drink with a stranger? Won't they gossip?'

I shrugged. 'So, where should we have a drink? Your home?'

He laughed uproariously, 'Naaah. Let's agree to meet in Delhi. On a regular basis. Or Shimla. I like Wildflower ... you?'

Wildflower. What was that? I didn't want 'That Man' to think I was ignorant. 'Oh ... wildflower ... yes ... sounds wonderful. When?'

He shrugged, 'Next week? Next month?'

'What about your wife? Ex? Girlfriend or is that girlfriends?'

'That Man' was already looking bored, but still staring at my nipples. 'You ask too many schoolgirlish questions, yaar ... what difference does it make? We can all become friends. Your husband included. He must be a nice guy.'

I was so confused! What was he saying? I sensed trouble ahead. And jumped right in, feet first! I sounded eager and needy and disgusting. 'Yes, yes, yes ... my husband ... I call him "Squirrel". He is a really nice guy. He doesn't mind anything. I mean, he is happy if I am happy—you know?'

'No. I don't know. And don't want to know. My dear, stop being tiresome and whiney ... either you are ready to fuck or you are not. Say it, yaar. Or else, all we have paid for is a martini for me ... and something stupid for you.'

My breasts were misbehaving again. The patches had grown and grown. 'Excuse me ... I need to go to the washroom and empty out some milk. Bye.' I was feeling flustered and silly. What on earth was I saying ... doing? I had to tell Squirrel about it right away.

'Am I doing something terrible? I mean, I haven't done it yet. But am definitely thinking about it,' I confessed in bed, with Squirrel's head nestling between my thighs.

He thought for a minute and said, 'I can book your Delhi ticket ... let me know. But take the baby with you, please. I can't breast feed.'

I shoved his head out of my crotch and yelled, 'You are so useless! I want to get out of it before I get into it ... and you want to buy my ticket!'

He looked lost and forlorn. 'Srilaaji, you don't understand. I want to go to Vancouver. There is nothing to live for here. I want to be with him, bas!' We were both hopelessly lost. But at least we had each other. Squirrel sobbed. I sobbed. The baby started wailing. My front buttoned blouses were only used for feeding a hungry mouth that wasn't my husband's.

Srilaaji's Fantasy

'That Man' asked me to get a friend along. 'I love threesomes.' I felt jealous—was I not enough? I told him I was a tigress in bed. He said, 'I need two bitches to amuse me.' He used the Hindi word—'kuttis'. I didn't feel insulted. In fact, I felt a shiver going down my spine. I wanted to be his kutti. But I didn't want another kutti around. He said I should try it ... two mouths are better than one. Then he counted all the available entry points, including ears. What? Ears, too? Yes, he said, ears have tunnels. Just like nostrils. He was right. Two women could lead an adventurous lover to many more places—their own secret crevices included.

Men didn't always know what to focus on and when. Though, 'That Man' was imaginative. He had a way with strawberries and cream and nipples and navels. I wanted to recreate the romance of Mughal-e-Azam ... with him stroking my naked body with an ostrich feather.

But he laughed. 'Give me a rider's crop instead.' I ordered one from the Riding Club. The jockey, who used to train Marwari bachchas, was tiny and cute. I invited him over to teach me how to use the slim whip. It made a whistling sound when I cracked it. And the welt it left looked beautiful on my skin. 'That Man' thought so as well. We loved our riding lessons. And asked the jockey to join in. Now there were four of us on a massive double bed. More mouths. More tunnels. So much to explore!

I took my time to set up a date in Delhi with 'That Man'. I wanted to meet in a small hotel. He preferred The Imperial. 'Don't be silly,' I protested. 'People will recognise us!'

He smiled, 'Let them! I thought you were gutsy and didn't care.'

I suggested an old, modest hotel in Connaught Place. 'Lousy bar … they don't know how to make good martinis.' It was decided then.

'Please use your own name … no stupid alibis,' he instructed. I was fine with that—Squirrel preferred it, too.

He had told me, 'I will tell the family you are going for social work … that way we can submit expenses also.' Squirrel was a practical man. Always thinking of saving money and 'additional kharcha' as he called it. I was learning from him. I had also started to cut back on additional kharcha.

Ma would have laughed at my new thrifty self. I had asked her once why she needed three Cartier watches and a dozen Chanel sunglasses. She had replied with a small laugh, 'It depends on the weather, Sweetie. Everything depends on the weather.' I wasn't sure whether or not she meant that comment in a deeply profound way. In a way, it does, doesn't it?

The weather had been cruel to my Ma. Buaji told me she was losing weight steadily, and her 'lungs were shrinking'. Whatever that meant. Of course, Babuji had hired the best nursing care for her, and brought in 'top

F.R.C.S. doctors' for consultation (as Buaji put it). I didn't think too much about her condition, and thought she had the usual cough-and-cold which most of us deal with round the year. We were all wrong. Even the 'top F.R.C.S. doctors'.

Ma had a relatively rare medical condition, and her lungs were shutting shop—but at a pace nobody could predict. Squirrel asked me if I needed to go to Kolkata ('Is she serious ... ?'). I had no reply.

'If she is not serious, let's wait. Why do double-double kharcha?' I was stupid enough to agree. When we finally decided to do the 'kharcha' and buy tickets, it was to attend Ma's funeral.

I think about Ma and her life a lot. What a lost and wasted life. I see those Cartier watches and Chanel sunglasses which are now with me, and feel so bad ... she was such a refined and elegant lady. Too well brought up to reveal her pain to anyone. Too well-mannered to complain. Too kind to utter a hurtful word. Buaji told me Ma's final request was to ask Buaji to dress her in a particular floral French chiffon saree ('Depending on the weather, of course'), and spray her favourite cologne ('4711'). She also wanted ivory roses 'in full bloom' ('Only if they are in season ...'), and had wondered if Buaji would be good enough to skip priests and such rituals? Would she consider a soft recitation of 'Gitanjali' please? And yes ... Vilayat Khan's recordings. Or Vivaldi's 'The Four Seasons', thank you.

I will never know what Babuji felt about Ma's passing. Well, I never knew what Babuji felt about her when she was living. Or about anything—births, deaths, existence. He was officially a widower now. But he had lived his entire life as one. Did Ma's death make even the slightest difference? Buaji told me he stopped eating nolen gurer sandesh after Ma died. It was the one sweet food item she broke her rules for, and actually relished. So did he. So, in a way, that was Babuji's way of mourning the death of a woman he barely had anything to do with when she was alive. He gave up his favourite dessert. I found it touching and true. Squirrel was not like Babuji, thank God. He was bhola and transparent. He really loved me. I loved him back, too. But I wouldn't ever give up nolen gurer sandesh for him. Or the lemon tarts from the Taj Patesserie, which were just heavenly.

I carried a box of strawberry tarts with me to Delhi, even though I knew 'That Man' avoided all things sugary or gooey. It was my way of showing love. He was out when I reached the hotel. I must have had a particularly guilty look on my face, even behind Ma's Cartier sunglasses. No. I remember now, they were Chanel, not Cartier. Anyway … I jumped out of my skin when the lovely girl at the reception desk—the one with the big boobs and almond eyes—asked, 'Mrs Khaitan? We have a suite for you … allow me …'

I muttered and said, 'Oh … a suite?' I was thinking of the 'additional kharcha'. The girl rechecked and said, 'Yes.

We have given you an upgrade.' I clutched my Bally bag (a gift from Squirrel), and followed Ms Huge Boobs mutely, watching her swing her shapely butt, as she strode ahead on three inch heels. I wondered if she shaved down there. She looked like the kind of woman who would. I didn't. And I had no way of knowing what 'That Man' preferred.

Left to myself in the beautiful suite, I studied every minute detail. I liked the mint green curtains and the veined marble in the bathroom was Italian. I wasn't sure what to do next, so I undressed, got into my pale blue nightie, and started solving a crossword puzzle from the newspaper placed on the side table. I ate some smoked almonds from a crystal jar, and stared at the crochet pattern of the coasters. There was nobody I could have asked important questions to about such meetings. 'That Man' was not a lover so far. But we had planned to alter that on this trip. What if he had changed his mind? I was beginning to feel really stupid! I had left my home, children and husband for ... for ... what? I soon found out for what.

I had fallen into a light sleep when I heard a knock. He was here! In my excitement to greet him, I scrambled out of bed and stubbed my big toe against a table. I let out a long wail and hopped on one leg to open the door. He was there, a Martini glass in hand, and a bunch of chrysanthemums in the other. He leaned forward so I could kiss him. I pecked his cheek, too flustered to react differently.

He took two steps back and asked, 'Is it raksha bandhan already? Am I your raakhi brother?' I was so ecstatic to see him, I jumped into his outstretched arms, and spilled the Martini.

He threw the chrysanthemums on the ash grey sofa, and offered me a sip of the remaining martini in the glass. 'Sorry ... I ate up the olives. How are you? And why are you wearing this nun-like, unsexy nightwear? Are your breasts still on tap? If so, I'd like to sample what's on offer.'

I pushed him away and stared hungrily at him. He walked around the suite inspecting every small thing. 'Let's do it in the bathroom,' he said firmly, leading me by the hand.

'Why not here? When there is a comfy bed?' I grumbled. 'I want you to be uncomfortable ... that's why. You are used to too many comforts ... it's too soft a life. Boring!'

He arranged towels on the marble floor and said, 'Go on ... lie down ...' Sensing my reluctance, he caught me by the shoulders and pushed till my knees buckled and I was kneeling, my face close to his groin.

'Let's start here ...' he said, unzipping himself. We started. And we didn't stop. No food. No water. No pause. I understood 'naked' for the first time. I never wanted to be dressed after that. Naked felt so good. 'That Man', born naked like all of us, had never needed to wear clothes-clothes like the rest of us 'boring' people. His naked self was all he had. His trump card. Now we were two naked people, comfortable in our nakedness. I was freed. And that night, on the cold, hard marble floor of an impersonal bathroom, in a strange city, with a man I barely knew, something changed for me. I knew who I was. And that woman was not my Ma. And would never be her. I thought about Khushboo—my little daughter. I didn't think of Kushal. Just Khushboo. She would have to take the trouble to know the naked me. And love that person. The bathroom floor had hurt me. I was bruised and aching. One day, Khushboo too might end up on a bathroom floor with a man she didn't know, but knew she loved. How would she deal with the discomfort? Three olives and a martini glass ... my world was complete.

I went back to Bombay the next morning. But I had left myself behind in Delhi. I had also left a precious bangle on the side table. It had been given to me by Ma when I turned 18. 'Sweetie ... this belonged to my Ma. Now it's yours. Make sure champagne spills on it. You are a big girl, now.' Champagne had indeed spilled on Ma's beautiful gold filigree bangle. Our post-love bingeing champagne.

At that moment, I missed Ma. I rarely missed her. But the presence of 'That Man' had changed many things for me. Maybe he had nothing to do with the changes. But I was feeling different. A little more alive, and a little more dead. Like Ma. Who was more dead than alive when she actually died. I didn't want my life to be like Ma's. I was not Ma. Which is why I was feeling so confused and troubled. There was nobody I could confide in. Bombay, with all its crowds and glamourous functions, made me feel lonely, even isolated. My children's lives interested me up to a point. I loved them and all that. But they couldn't compensate for my aloneness. Neither could sweet Squirrel.

I met him over tea and onion kachoris, after my Delhi trip. 'Srilaaji ... you don't look happy. He wasn't nice to you?'

I smiled. It was such a trusting question. 'Maybe, he was too nice,' I replied, lying to myself and to Squirrel.

He brightened up immediately, 'Oh good! I was worried. Sometimes men can be ... can be ...' I didn't hasten to provide the apt adjective. I didn't have one that applied to 'That Man.' In fact, I was looking for one to describe myself. What was I? Who had I become?

'Let's buy a home in Delhi,' I told Squirrel, who was about to eat his third kachori.

'Oh ... but I don't have a business in Delhi ... what will I tell the family?'

I thought for a bit, 'Just say I have a lot of social work commitments in Delhi ... work has increased. I need to go there twice or thrice a month. Getting a home will work out cheaper than staying in 5-star hotels. It will save money in the long run also ... airline ticket prices are going up all the time. We'll be cutting back on additional kharcha.'

Squirrel was thoughtful, like he was doing mental

arithmetic. 'That's true. Why do additional kharcha? You are right, Srilaaji ... I will talk about it at the office tomorrow. Srilaaji, you are a genius. And that purple colour looks very good on you. But don't mind Srilaaji ... I can see bites and teeth marks on your neck. You know ... all the ladies will notice ... please use a shawl when you come to dinner.'

I nodded, and touched my bites ... his teeth were known to my body. They were a part of me. I looked at Squirrel, picked up an embroidered napkin (yellow roses in cross stich), and tenderly wiped kachori crumbs from the corner of his mouth.

'You are a good man, Squirrel,' I said sincerely. He blushed, stared at his toes and said, 'Srilaaji, I love you ... bas.'

I turned to go to my room. Then I turned around and said, 'Three Olives'. Squirrel looked bewildered. 'That's what we'll call our Delhi home,' I stated flatly and smiled.

~

'That Man' had disappeared after our Delhi trip. It had been decided we wouldn't call or try to stay in touch. If we were to meet, he would contact me and set up the entire thing—city, timing, duration. Two months passed. One of the ways I tried to distract myself was by feeding stray dogs. I carried packets of Glucose biscuits in my car, and told the driver to stop whenever I spotted a stray mongrel. Soon all the strays in my area began to run behind my car, barking and wagging their tails.

I was called the 'Kutteywali madam'. And all I wanted was to be 'That Man's kutti'. I had started to wilt and look wan. My mother-in-law noticed and asked pointedly, 'Third one? Don't tell me! I know a good gynae ...' If she only knew! Or maybe she did. These Marwari in-laws know everything. I looked away guiltily and hastily denied any such thing.

I almost said, 'We don't sleep together any longer—your sweet son and I,' but kept mum. I changed the topic and asked her about the flower show on the Raj Bhavan lawns. 'Yes ... very nice, very nice. We take a lot of trouble over our flowers. You should join our Bonsai society.' Artificially stunted trees! Not for me. Our lives and growth were stunted enough.

'Khushboo and Kushal have been crying a lot these days. Maybe you should spend more time with them,' she said pointedly.

'Yes,' I replied, 'Maybe.'

'Where's your gold bangle? The one your beloved mother had given you?' I touched my wrist, as if I had just discovered it was missing. 'Oh ... that one? I have kept it safely.'

She raised an eyebrow, 'That's fine ... do wear it again. Your wrist looks bare without it.'

'That Man' had located and retrieved the bangle the next day itself. And kept it. I felt honoured it was with him. As if a bit of me was in his possession. It made me feel connected and happy. I wanted him to keep it forever. Like, that would make me a part of him forever. I had no idea when we would meet again or even where.

One afternoon, a delivery boy came to the mansion with a small packet. He told the durwan, it had to be handed over personally to me and nobody else, since it was a piece of jewellery I had ordered. I instantly knew it was from him. I tore open the cardboard carton and there, nestled between kesar barfis, was a small note. 'Martinis at the Oberoi Bar. Delhi. Friday. 7 p.m.' My heart was dangling from the neem tree, and screeching parrots were about to eat it. I wanted to kiss the delivery boy. At least, hold him close and thank him. I gave him 500 rupees (the barfi cost 200), and rushed into my room to read and reread and reread that one line.

Squirrel was still at work. My tickets had to be booked! What if every single seat was taken on Friday? Delhi flights were always heavily booked. What if I couldn't get on that plane? Train! That's it. I would leave on a train. Take the one on Thursday night. And arrive in Delhi well ahead of the scheduled hour. Hotel! Squirrel would have to move fast and get me a gorgeous room. I completely forgot I had organised a children's party for Kushal's third birthday on Friday. The invitations had gone out, the Mickey Mouse cake ordered. Balloon man and joker booked. I had to get out of it, somehow, anyhow. But how? Squirrel would know what to do.

And he did! I told him about the barfi and the birthday and everything. I was crying. He wiped my tears with his initialed handkerchief. 'Srilaaji ... leave it to me. I will handle everything. You just go.'

I hugged him tight. 'You are my savior, Squirrel,' I cried. He held me close, kissed the top of my head and said simply, 'No, Srilaaji ... you are wrong. It is the other way around.'

My regular masseuse, Shaku, was scheduled to arrive the same evening. My heart was still dangling from the neem tree. Shaku was a wise, dignified middle-aged Maharashtrian woman who used to be a proficient midwife till her gnarled hands refused to deliver babies as efficiently as they once did. She switched to massaging memsaabs in Malabar Hill and earned much more for a few hours of work than sweating it out with full-term women taking their time to push, push, push. I liked Shaku and she liked me. I knew that from the way she stayed a few extra minutes and offered a head massage for free, though I was only paying for a full body massage.

Today, she sensed my distress and asked softly if I was feeling unwell. Whhhhhoooooosh! Out came everything in a mad gush. I told her I had fallen in love with a married man who was a rascal. She poured jasmine oil into a steel container and asked me to lie down on my stomach. This way, I could keep talking without being able to check her expression. I didn't spare a single detail. I had been dying to talk about 'That Man' to someone—anyone!

I was so stupidly in love, I had 'confessed' everything to baby Khushboo while feeding her tiny bits of aloo parathas fried in pure ghee. She had babbled on and laughed happily. I had laughed with her.

Now my daughter and I were a part of a conspiracy. It was our secret. Even though she hadn't understood a word. I felt the same way talking to Shaku. What would this illiterate lady know about our kind of lives? My secret was perfectly safe with her.

After I had finished gushing, she stopped kneading my neck muscles to ask, 'What does he do besides breaking up marriages?' I was shocked by her boldness, but wanted to hear more. I fed her a little information—how much did I know about him, anyway?

I told her about my Delhi trip and she tut-tutted, 'He should come to Bombay to meet you. Do you know your own status? Your own position? You are the Chhoti Bhabhiji of this well-known family. Please think about your husband, your children. And that fellow sounds useless, like a loafer, a nobody. You are too good for him.'

I told her in a small voice that I was helpless. 'I love him too much. I will leave all this if he asks me to.' Shaku used a hot towel and started to rub the soles of my feet.

'Madam ... your husband may kill him. In our community men like that are killed, to save the family's honour.'

I sighed, 'My husband would not kill a mosquito that was sucking his blood. Forget this man.' Shaku, who knew every fold and crevice in my body, asked me to turn over. Then she lifted my torso and made me sit up.

'Madam ... what is that man's "aukat" that he dares to sleep with someone from your background? He is a nobody. A nothing. In our community, such a man would be tracked down and murdered by the menfolk. Madam, it is a question of the family's honour. If not your husband, your brother-in-law may organise the killing.'

At which point, I burst out laughing, 'Shaku, we are Marwaris. These are Marwari men! There is no money to be made in this case. What will anybody gain by killing my lover? Nothing! We are not Rajputs! Those men do silly things like killing for honour. Do you know something? If a crow comes and eats up a grape from my husband's plate, he will feel terrible about one grape being taken by the crow. Our men count the grapes in every bunch—force of habit. If he catches the crow, which is impossible, he will wonder if there are any buyers for such a clever crow. We Marwaris buy and sell. We don't kill.'

Shaku kept quiet. 'Madam, it is none of my business ... but please don't destroy your home for this worthless man.'

She had described 'That Man' as 'worthless'. But to me he was priceless. No force on earth could keep me from meeting him. Wherever, however. Besides, I had a strong ally in Squirrel. He was my insurance cover if anything went wrong in the future. In fact, I wanted Squirrel and 'That Man' to become friends someday. I was sure they would get along and then we could all be together without anybody raising eyebrows.

I proposed this to 'That Man' when we met in Delhi. He dismissed the suggestion and laughed uproariously. 'Listen Bhabhiji ... you keep your sweet husband to yourself, please. I have no interest in meeting him. Besides, what makes you think I will stay interested in you? At the moment, you are a good diversion. My tea business goes through ups and downs, depending on how the auctions go. It's down right now. I need to take my mind off the first flush and nonsense like that. I like your breasts. You turn up when I need you. You are not fussy and demanding. You don't expect gifts. You go away quietly. You pay all the bills. It works for me.'

I was hanging on to his every word. Memorising everything he said. It was important! I now knew what he expected, what he didn't like, what he appreciated. I would try my best to please him and improve on my responses in future.

I started obsessing over his wife. I told him I wanted to see a photograph ... perhaps even meet her, as he had suggested earlier. First, the wife, then his mistress, after that all his casual girlfriends. I wanted to know if I had anything in common with them. There had to be something! Big breasts? Small waist? Tight vaginas? Curly hair? Large teeth? But he flatly refused.

'Forget it, Bhabhiji ...' he said as we lay against the large pillows of what had now become our 'regular' suite at the Oberoi. I asked him why he called me 'Bhabhiji'? Did he harbor sister-in-law fantasies?

He replied, 'I call all Marwari ladies Bhabhijis ... nobody suspects anything if I address them respectfully.'

'So, how many Bhabhijis have you known?' He looked thoughtful, then started to count on his fingers.

'Stop!' I cried.

He carried on, 'I think you know three of them. Lovely ladies. But bitchy and greedy. Even in bed.' Was he saying all this to torment me? Or did these women get more pieces of him—the best slices? The biggest share? I asked him his wife's name.

He smiled, 'It's too personal to just give out ... that too, to a stranger.' I was a stranger? We had slept together twelve times by then. Yes, twelve. Not counting making love twice and thrice in one night. I had a head for numbers. And I kept track.

'Stranger?' I squeaked, my voice barely emerging from my throat.

'Why? You thought something else? Shut up and suck me ... you talk too much.'

'That Man' was absolutely right. I talked too much. I thought too much. I felt too much. It was really my fault. How was he to blame for my shortcomings? I asked Squirrel, 'Do you think I talk too much?'

He just hugged me and said, 'I can never get enough of your voice. Even when you scream at me, or scream at the children. You always sound very sweet to me, Srilaaji.'

Squirrel had started dropping the children to play school, collecting them, and attending all the parents-teacher meetings. He was like any other 'school mother', and had made friends with several ladies he met during all the activity days. I was so happy for him. He still talked about Soumitro and his betrayal. But the pain was less now. Squirrel cried from time to time, thinking of their happy times together, especially if someone in his vicinity smoked Soumitro's brand of cigarettes, or if he heard Bengali songs, recognised Soumitro's fragrance on another man.

I felt it was time for Squirrel to fall for someone else. But I wasn't expecting him to fall for one of the mothers from Kushal's batch. 'We take piano lessons together. And we meet at the race course for riding class. That's all.'

I was surprised. 'I didn't know you play the piano. Or ride.'

Squirrel hastened to clarify, 'No no no, Srilaaji, the children take lessons. We only supervise ...'

I screamed, 'What is all this "we-we" nonsense? Now all of a sudden you have become "we" with some other woman? I thought we were the only "we".'

Squirrel blushed, stammered and said, 'Srilaaji ... it is not like that. Mitaliji is a very nice lady. Very refined. Dancer types. Bharat Natyam. Our Khusboo should also learn from her when she's older. She has a small school at her home. It's not that far ... Nepean Sea road.'

I grabbed Squirrel by his jacket collar (nice wool and

silk suit from Savile Row). 'Have you gone mad? Mitalji! Why are you calling this woman "ji"?'

Squirrel squirmed, 'I call you "ji", too.'

I yelled, 'Exactly! I thought I was the only woman in your life. The only woman you called "ji" out of love and respect ... now this! Does she also call you Squirrel? If the answer is "yes" I will divorce you tomorrow, and you can marry that prostitute ... dance bar girl.'

'Please listen to me, Srilaaji ... please.' Squirrel was whimpering and pleading, 'She is not a dance bar girl. Mitaliji is a classical dancer. She danced at NCPA once. Group dance. And you cannot divorce me. Marwaris don't divorce, okay?'

My chest was heaving, and my eyes, bulging. I needed to sit down. 'Marwaris don't divorce, huh? No ... of course, they don't! They are the world's biggest hypocrites. Marriage is like a life sentence. Once married, you are condemned to your seven-star cell. Wellllll ... Mr Squirrel, let me tell you one thing, in case you don't know it already. I am not like those other Marwari wives. If I feel I cannot take this life anymore, I will leave you ... walk out! Quick march. No looking back. I don't want to live a miserable life like my Ma. I don't want to be like those fake women I meet at the club, who only discuss handbags and diamonds. I have dreams ... big dreams. I will show you, Mr Squirrel ... so please don't act over-smart with me!'

Squirrel was sobbing and tears were falling tup tup

tup on the starched tray cloth with tiny embroidered violets. A few tears fell into the small bowl holding the paani puri ka paani.

I pointed an accusatory finger at it, 'See what you are doing ... ruining the paani puri!' Squirrel started to mop up what he could, though there were no stains in sight. I checked my breathlessness, sipped water, and continued in my frostiest voice, 'What a cry baby you are! Has your "Mitaliji" seen you like this? She will run away! Let me meet this Mitali ... I will teach her a few new steps! Bharat Natyam ki bachchi!'

Squirrel stammered, 'Srilaaji ... please ... leave her out of this! Poor thing ... what is her fault? She is so lonely and neglected ... she needs love and companionship.'

I threw a Lalique lion at Squirrel's head. It missed and crashed on the marble floor.

Squirrel yelped, 'Srilaaji! What have you done! It's a Lalique! Not some sasta crystal. It is Anushreeji's favourite! Even Khusboo and Kushal love it!'

I stared at the glass scattered on the marble and cursed Mitali, 'May her heart be shredded by glass even sharper than these pieces.' Then came my final cut, 'Have you screwed Mitali? No, na? Then? Can't, na? Still thinking of Soumitro, na? Come on, Squirrel—time barbaad mat karo.'

Mitali's name was never mentioned again. I lost interest in her. And the piano/horse riding lessons continued as before. Squirrel had learnt a lesson.

Women were not for him. He'd be an ass to try such a stunt again.

~

My visits to Delhi took a slight detour, which had nothing to do with 'That Man'. I had met a few people quite by chance while staying at the hotel. I had hours to myself, waiting for my lover to turn up. I'd spend them in the lobby, sipping tea and flipping through magazines. Occasionally, regulars would make eye contact, nod and smile. Some would say politely, 'How are you, madam? Enjoying Dilli?' I would nod and go back to reading *Femina* or *Stardust*.

After a while, I made 'breakfast friends'—those who had fixed tables and ordered eggs Benedict. They were the posh people, who were fussy about the marmalade and asked for carrot and orange juice 'chilled and strained'. All of us dressed up for breakfast as if we were acting in a James Ivory film. There were always fancy foreigners present—rich British tourists on their 'empire still exists' nostalgia tours. They used to actually say 'Koi hai', to attract the attention of liveried bearers.

All of us carried two newspapers (*Hindustan Times* and *The Times of India*) to show we were well-informed and politically aware. I rarely read mine. But I could guess the news well enough by just eavesdropping conversations, conducted in hushed tones. Occasionally, I would spot a few ministers and parliamentarians huddled in discreet alcoves, and talking to men in safari suits, possibly, business people from out of town, cutting shady deals.

One such 'Safari Suit' walked up to me while I was enjoying my milky cappuccino, and introduced himself, 'Namastey, Madamji! Myself Dheeraj Sharma, businessman. Your good name? I am seeing you, Madamji. Regular visitor. You are also doing business?'

I was listless that morning ... our love making the night before had been devoid of real sex-sex—that is, I had failed to please 'That Man', even though I had tried very hard, and not objected to those stupid sex toys he liked. He had taken to calling me 'K.K.'—short for 'Khaitan Kutti'. I had got the feeling his interest in our sexual bond was waning, even though I refused him nothing.

He'd said, 'Listen yaar K.K. you need to do something new in bed ... you are too boring!' I had sat up and climbed on top of him, my breasts nuzzling his face. He had moved away and snarled, 'You are smothering me ... I can't breathe!' He switched on the television set and started calculating his losses while watching a business channel. 'Shit! Another hit ... that Big Bull is full of bullshit. I should never have gone with his fucking market tips—bloody ass. Making a complete bandar of all of us ...'

His calculations were going wrong on several other levels as well. And our fractured life together was looking like it was about to collapse. That's when I had a brainwave. 'How much do you need to cover your losses?' His eyes were shining as he grabbed my shoulders and turned to face me, 'What? K.K., are you saying you can help? I need a short term loan—that's all. Even the bloody tea auctions have been the worst in years. I am not worried ... things will turn around ... but at the moment I could do with a little something.'

I purred, 'How much?' He grabbed my breasts and stuck his tongue into my mouth, 'As much as you can spare, K.K.' I felt triumphant! And stupidly grateful. He was ready to take my money—how wonderful. It was nothing short of an honour. I felt as if he had fished me out of a deep and dark pool before I drowned. In a way, he had! I was saved! At least for the time being. He needed me! Oh, how fantastic! 'That Man' needed me! It was more than enough. He wouldn't drop me from his life. I sent up a small prayer to the Big Bull—keep those bogus market tips going ... let him lose more money at the stock exchange. Let the country's economy collapse. Let all the tea plantations in Darjeeling dry up and wither because of frost. I was there to stand by 'That Man'—no matter what the cost.

But the reality of my rash promise made in bed had only just started to hit me. Where would I get the money from? I didn't have an independent income, and the pocket money I received from Squirrel was hardly enough to pay some of my bills. Squirrel had the money.

But I wasn't sure he'd give it to me to hand over to the unreliable man I was sleeping with. This was on my mind when Safari Suit approached me. God knows what I sensed about him, but I certainly sensed it—he was the ticket I was looking for. Yes, this oily stranger chewing paan masala and staring at me up and down, up and down. He was the number one opportunity, and opportunity had walked right up to me.

I looked at him and smiled. 'Sit?' I said, patting the chair next to mine. 'Tea? Coffee?'

He moved swiftly, sat down and said, 'Water. Only water. I don't drink tea, coffee, cold drinks ...' I smiled some more, 'How sweet! What about milk? Lassi?' He shook his head, 'Madamji ... thank you, ji, but only water.' And that's how we started by clinking glasses of non-refrigerated water, in the lobby of a hotel, where I regularly met and fucked a man who did not love me. I needed another man's money, to keep the first man from leaving me. For that, I was willing to go to any lengths with a third man, a complete stranger ... and I did.

Safari Suit and I hit it off instantly. He was what was called a 'liaison officer'—the go-between. A fixer. Delhi was full of them. Sleazy fellows in stinky safari suits whose sole job was to bribe whosoever, from clerks to ministers, on behalf of clients who needed government contracts passed. These men worked exceedingly hard at developing 'contacts' (which they pronounced as 'cuntacts'—appropriately, as it turned out). They knew the system and how exactly it worked. In this fellow's case, he specialised in getting clearances for large government projects—factories, roads, housing societies, dams. His clients were faceless, anonymous moneybags, who paid him fat fees for pushing files up the food chain, till they reached the P.A. who worked for the targeted ministersaab. After that, another set of middle men took over.

Safari Suit had spotted a bait in me—for those men. The ones who reached the minister and had access to influential bureaucrats in different ministries. Safari Suit didn't waste time spelling out what he was looking for. 'Madamji, you are from a good, respectable khaandaan. You can open doors for me, just by using your name and making a few phone calls. That's all.' He didn't want to sleep with me—he said that, too. 'Madamji, I am a family man—wife, three children. I don't do all this other bad stuff, supplying women and all that. That is called a "ganda cheez ka dhanda". I am not a pimp, Madamji, I am not a bhadwa. My business is clean. I make intros ... that's all. If you agree, we can make many intros together—the sky is the limit, madamji! I'm telling you ...' I tried to ignore the sweaty hand he reached out to clinch our arrangement. The paan masala breath was making me gag.

When I didn't shake his outstretched hand, he withdrew it hastily. 'Okay then ... bye, madamji ... here's my card. If you change your mind, call me. My wife's name is Madhura—she has a sweet voice. You just say Bombaywalli behenji, if she asks your name. I will understand.'

Three weeks later, we found ourselves in the coffee shop, talking turkey. I had decided to give this a chance, after discussing it with Squirrel. 'Srilaaji, you are so charming. Who can say "no" to you?' Squirrel had commented encouragingly. I needed Squirrel's green signal. I now had it. There I was ready to pick up the phone with men I barely knew, to set up appointments for a man I barely knew, so that another man I barely knew could benefit! For me to succeed, I needed Squirrel's support and calling card. I also needed to make myself known independently.

Squirrel had a great idea. 'Why don't you host a charity event—a fundraiser for educating woh gareeb ladkis ... you know, those girls from the jhopadpattis? I will arrange a minister to inaugurate the show, and you can call rich people, presswallas ... leave it to me! We can name the charity after my grandmother. That way, the other family members also won't object.'

All this to hang on to 'That Man', who had been incommunicado for a while, bluntly saying, 'Forget it, K.K. ... I'm screwed ... so how do you expect me to screw? Not in the mood. Call me when you have the money ... I need money, not sex.'

I was determined to get him back in my life, and this was one of the easier options. I had thought of pledging my wedding jewellery, but that would have involved the family. I tried to sell one of my big stone rings—the one Squirrel's mother had given me on a wedding anniversary saying, 'Very expensive. Six carats ... look after it.' But it had turned out to be a dud. A poor quality Hong Kong diamond—size without value. Like so many other things in that mansion.

If I worked hard on the charity event, got some artist friends from Kolkata and Bombay to donate their paintings, I could raise the money I needed to get 'That Man' back in my life. I asked the friendly Public Relations' lady at the hotel to help me with the guest list. By now, I was known to most of the staff and had established good relationships with a few. Each time I arrived from Bombay, I would bring small gifts—mithai or almond rocks from the Taj. Preeti, the P.R. lady was most helpful and shared her list willingly, offering to introduce me to florists and card designers. She also negotiated a good rate for hosting the event by the poolside.

Squirrel was thrilled and impressed. 'Srilaaji ... I always tell you, nobody can say "no" to you.' I asked him to shut up and make a few calls to VIPs.

Squirrel looked puzzled, 'Srilaaji, everybody in Delhi is a VIP ... I will call only VVIPs, the ones with bodyguards. When they attend a party, it looks very impressive.'

Even if I say so myself, my event turned out so fantastic, so fantastic, that strangers in the hotel lobby walked up to congratulate me. The press covered it well, but kept calling me a 'Bombay socialite'. Squirrel was pleased. 'Srilaaji, they are paying you a compliment ... what is wrong in being called a socialite? It means you are rich and glamourous. Soon you will be famous, also. After that happens—wah! Ministers will be at your feet.'

Squirrel's words were prophetic. One minister fell hard for me and also fell at my feet—he told Safari Suit to arrange a private meeting. 'I will give her whatever she wants,' he said. Safari Suit was a little embarrassed conveying the message. But his file was stuck for three years in this man's ministry, and if I 'did the needful', we'd both make a lot of money. I needed the money for 'That Man', who had gone back to living with his wife, since he couldn't afford hotels any longer! I agreed to meet the creepy minister.

'Madam ... you are too beautiful ... too much you are, madam,' the man gushed. I thought he was going to faint.

I sucked in my breath and stuck out my breasts, 'Jhoota!' I said, making my voice all flirty and low. His body went into spasms and he started to giggle uncontrollably. 'Madam, you are better than top-top film actress ... too much beauty you are.' I licked my lips.

He lunged for me. I took a step back ... he stumbled and fell ... not at my feet, but on them. 'Sorrrrry ...' I said throatily, as he got up unsteadily. His hands were unzipping the fly of his polyester trousers. 'Madam ...

madam …' he was groaning and bleating. I held his shoulders and steadied him. 'Let's talk tomorrow … I will contact you. Nothing happens today, okay? Namastey.' That was enough for now. No money, no free touch.

I spoke to Safari Suit in my sternest voice, 'Don't waste my time in future. I need to see some cash first … why should I bother to meet this rakshas—for free?'

Safari Suit hastened to clarify, 'Madam Sir … please don't say like that. I feel dukh. Very, very dukh. Let us meet tomorrow only, Madam Sir.' I had been promoted. From Madamji to Madam Sir. Good. This doggie needed to be kept on a tight leash. I abhorred Delhi, and to be there without bedding 'That Man'? Total time-waste. I went for a long walk to Lodhi Garden in search of my bleeding heart—was it hanging from that Peepul tree in the distance? I was feeling intensely sorry for myself. What the hell was I doing? For whom? An unworthy lout of a man? I thought earlier I was the lucky bitch with an understanding, loving and rich husband, two lovely children, and what is called a great 'set up' in Bombay. But look at the way things had turned out?

Squirrel was just fine in the mansion, with his family and our kids. He had many friends at different levels—his club friends, golfing friends, old school friends, assorted cousins who were friends, and now all those PTA mothers who adored him and brought dabbas with his favourite snacks to school. Squirrel was loved. And me? A desperate and miserable woman hanging around, clad in diaphanous sarees, hoping to gain special entry into the closed club of Lutyens' Dehli. I had a safari suit clad pimp (no other word for what he did), and a few newly acquired 'friends' whose wives were insecure and suspicious, since I was always alone. If they only knew my heart (and lower down) were spaces reserved for just one person, they would not have been this nervous. I didn't care a hoot for the ghastly men these bouffant-wali society ladies were married to.

My eyes were perpetually vacant ... constantly searching for 'That Man' in the strangest of places. Lodhi Gardens was the ideal venue to bump into influential people, I'd been told. They walked and walked, round and round, but mostly in silence. All of them had at least twenty people walking with them, even if they were not with them. The prime walkers wearing starched khadi, expensive sneakers, and priceless shawls, with heavily armed bodyguards were the really important ones—I recognised them from their pictures in the newspapers Some were ministers, others superstar Supreme Court lawyers and judges. What was I supposed to do to attract their attention?

I started running. Yes, running, not walking. Always at the same time, and as close to their groups as possible. I looked sexy in running clothes and my breasts bounced and bounced—so much, in fact, that dogs got startled and started barking as I bounced past them. The men noticed—oh yes, they did! I noticed them noticing me, and felt pleased. But this attention was useless unless I cut a deal, with or without Safari Suit.

I sought Squirrel's advice and his response was swift. 'Srilaaji, actually you need me in Delhi to do your work properly. People there are not comfortable with women without husbands by their side. They feel uncomfortable, and avoid such ladies. You know ... it is true ... blackmail and all that. Single ladies are a big, big danger to society. If these men see me with you, they will feel more relaxed. We will get proper invitations to proper parties. That is the correct method.' He was right.

We now had a home in Delhi. It was easy to divide our time. Squirrel was beginning to enjoy the power games that are uniquely Delhi, and the ladies seemed to love him. He considered bringing the children and moving here. I was not for it at all. Khushboo and Kushal enjoyed their Bombay life, had made good school friends and were very popular. Why uproot them? Squirrel agreed, and soon we were making steady inroads into Delhi society, where I was referred to as 'that Marwari socialite from Bombay'. I decided to fix that. Squirrel was simply labelled, 'Marwari moneybags', and it didn't upset him. 'So what, Srilaaji? Better to be called moneybags than kadka, na? I'm telling you Srilaaji, these Dilliwalis are just jealous of you. Of us! Sab log jaltey hain.' The family didn't mind our being away from Bombay. All the businesses were doing well, and Squirrel's mother was relieved not to have to deal with me—the kitchen and tijori were all hers.

I missed the intensity of Bombay. It remained Bombay to me, even after it became 'Mumbai'. It made such a difference! 'I live in Bombay' sounded so much sexier than 'I live in Mumbai'! After the first few years of detesting Bombay, I had become a 'Bombaywali', in sync with its madness. It was a city that kept you on the edge, pushing, pushing, pushing. I missed its hectic pace and rough ways. I missed the mad mixture of languages that somehow were understood by all. But my sights were set beyond the edge of Bombay's Arabian Sea, beyond its coast. I had a different vision for myself. I had discovered power. Individual power—I liked the feeling. Even if my heart remained powerless, because of one man. It had been four months of no contact. I was beginning to think I would never meet him again. Maybe he was dead. How would I know? Nobody would inform me. Maybe his wife was dead? In which case, I could marry him. There were nights I would scratch myself all over, till the skin broke and I would bleed. Squirrel would rush to get ice from the refrigerator and tenderly wipe the beads of bright red blood dotting my arms and legs like a temporary tattoo.

My every breath was dedicated to 'That Man'—it seemed so normal! And now, I had started to make money. Not much, but enough to demonstrate my commitment to save him. But how could I save him if I didn't know where he was? At one point, I thought of hiring a detective. Squirrel discouraged me and said it would show me in a poor light. He told me to focus on 'artistic things' and 'charity', explaining it was a good thing to be seen as a patron of the arts.

'Srilaaji ... all this art-shaart is important. You host exhibitions—I will back you. See also how art is selling! Good investment ... better than stock market.' I had started enjoying art in a genuine way, and we used to visit all the major art openings ... it was also a good place to meet politicians and other prominent people. Our photographs started appearing regularly in society pages, and soon photographers began calling out to me by name! Frankly, I used to feel thrilled when they chorused, 'Srilaaji, Srilaaji ... this way, ma'am ... to your right, ma'am. It was while I was busy posing in front of a large Satish Gujral, that I saw 'That Man'.

I froze.

No. I died.

My heart stopped temporarily. And my brain shut down. I felt numbness in my limbs, as I held on to Squirrel for support. I thought I was going to faint. My eyes shut on their own. My mouth was dry. Someone was offering water. All I wanted was his touch. I could smell him. Hear him. Even though he wasn't anywhere close. Tears of joy were pouring down my cheeks ... as I walked towards him blindly. I saw nothing else, and nobody else. His back was to me ... that back! Were my scratch marks still there? The many bites on his shoulders? I had told him I would mark him for life. Scar him!

He had laughed and said, 'So long as you don't

damage my nu-nu …' There was a small crowd around him, as photographers rushed to go click, click, click. What? Had he suddenly become that famous? How? Before I could reach him, he had moved swiftly in the opposite direction, and was close to the exit, with the photographers still trailing him. Whose name were they calling out? His? Since when had he changed his name to Bunty?

'Who's Bunty?' I asked the first person I met, one of the ladies from the Delhi Gymkhana. She looked surprised, 'You should know! I mean, you are the Bombay socialite … and you are asking a pucca Dilliwali, "Who's Bunty?"' She rolled her eyes, 'Bunty is just the biggest thing to have happened to Bollywood! Didn't you watch her debut film? My God, kasam se yaar … don't know which world you live in. She's a babe, man, a real babe! Hottttt. Like a tawa.'

I had not noticed the woman. Imagine. I had gone blind. I did not see a thing beyond his shoulders and the back of his head … an inch of his neck, with stray curly hair grazing his shirt collar. That's all. Nothing else. His hair had grown a little. I spotted more grey. Poor chap. Must have been the stress. His jacket was of a different cut, not like the jackets I was so familiar with. This jacket was shorter, tighter. Had checks. Checks! He hated checks. I couldn't see his legs too clearly in that crush. But I think he was wearing jeans. Blue jeans. Another shock. He had stated grandly, 'I am a boxwallah … a tea man. A Bengali. We dress like gentlemen in upper class British clubs. Jeans are for labourers.'

What had happened? I know! Bunty had happened.

I leaned on Squirrel and whispered hoarsely, 'That was him!' Squirrel held me tightly, and whispered back, 'I know!' He guided me to the exit ... we were walking on the same path he had taken minutes earlier. I was sure I could still smell him ... it was a trail I knew so well. Squirrel was holding me securely. I felt safe in his embrace. But I was only, only, only longing ... no dying ... for 'That Man'.

'Let's change the name of our Delhi bungalow, Squirrel,' I said that night, as we cuddled on the gigantic four poster post. 'Srilaaji ... Three Olives is a nice name. I was thinking we could start a restaurant by the same name.' He really didn't get it, my sweet, loving, stupid Squirrel. It wasn't about the name. It was about him. I wanted to get back to Bombay, I had decided to change myself.

Starting with Squirrel's family and my children. I would become the ideal Marwari bahu and go shopping with my mother-in-law. I would go to the spa with my sisters-in-law and their tiresome girlfriends. I would become a full time 'volunteer mom' at my children's school and organize a class picnic to the zoo. I would buy my father-in-law personalised stationery. There were many things I could do to forget 'That Man'. But I failed. I couldn't think of anything else. I became obsessed with Bunty. I had to summon Shaku for an unscheduled massage. I needed to hear it from her.

'That Bunty is a maha chaalu cheez,' Shaku assured me, as she worked on my pulsating temples. 'Every hero has had sambhyog with her.'

'What is sambhyog?' I asked. 'Bhabhiji—s-e-x—I cannot say that word.' I visualised 'That Man' and Bunty in bed, and my body revolted. I got up and went to puke. 'Don't waste your ulti on that fellow, Bhabhiji ... even your ulti has value. He is a full zero.'

Squirrel had said, 'Srilaaji, you are safe with me.'

I should have screamed, 'Idiot! I don't want to be safe! I hate being safe ... I like danger. And I only want to be with him. Do something! If you really love me, you will find him and bring him to me.' I confessed this thought to Shaku.

She slapped my bare buttocks and snorted, 'Hattttt! You want to make your husband into a eunuch? What will the world say? They will call him a hijda. Or worse, a bhadwa. You want to be a hijda's wife, huh? If your husband loves you and wants to keep you, there is only one honorable thing for him to do—he has to kill that gunda.'

I started to cry, 'If he dies—I die.' Shaku shook me hard, 'Wake up, Bhabhiji! You are under a spell. We have a man in our village who breaks such spells. I can ask him to come here and cure you. It will cost five thousand rupees. But at least you will get your mind back.'

I stared at Shaku and my eyes lit up. 'Then this same man must have the power to cast a spell on Bunty? Or her lover? Or both? I can pay! He must destroy their affair and get him back to me.'

Shaku slapped her own forehead and exclaimed, 'Hey Devaa ... how do I drill some sense into your bheja? Even if he leaves Bunty he won't come back to you. Why? Because he does not love you!'

I screamed, 'Liar! You are a wicked woman. I hate you! Black tongued witch! Of course, he loves me! What would you know, you slumwali ghati. Here ... take your money and get out. Don't ever come back again.'

Shaku's black tongue had done its job. My limited peace was destroyed, and I started eating and eating everything in sight. Including our mandir ka prasad. The cook had taken to glaring at me, each time I stepped into his territory. I heard him complaining, 'Bhabhiji pagal ho gayi hai. Today, she asked for a ghee paratha, she added a big lump of gur on top of it, then poured honey, and sprinkled chopped walnuts over the whole thing. I couldn't believe it! She adds strands of Kashmiri saffron to her honey milk. Two dibbas are finished! What do I tell the maalkin?'

The 'maalkin', my mother-in-law was pleasantly surprised to see me in the kitchen. 'Oh ... what are you doing here? I thought you were in Delhi organising another charity event. Very nice, very nice, very nice. A lot of punya will come your way.'

I looked at her guiltily and tried to hide the ghee

paratha. I wasn't sure whether she was being sarcastic or sincere. 'The babalog are doing well, their school reports came yesterday. You must have seen them?' I hadn't. I lied and said I had.

'Khushboo needs additional help. She may need braces ... her teeth are emerging in their own way, here and there and not in a line. Kushal needs help, too. The class teacher was a little worried—his speech is not very clear. Maybe you can take an appointment with a speech therapist? I know a good one at Gowalia Tank.' I heard her, but I didn't.

'Yes ... his Hindi is weak,' I replied confidently. My mind was on Bunty and her picture in the papers. She was dressed for the premiere of her next film, clad in a figure hugging fishtail gown ... and beaming next to her was 'That Man' wearing a sharp tux. He was described as the producer of the film. Producer? What producer? Where did he get the money from? And wearing a tux? Since when? What happened to the boxwalla Bong snob? He resembled a bandwalla in his penguin suit. Bunty looked like she needed to head to the nearest haystack and be properly ravaged. But not by him.

Srilaaji's Fantasy

Bunty is under a waterfall with swans fighting to make love to her. She is enjoying the experience and her eyes are shut. She opens her mouth and fresh strawberries emerge. She sticks one inside her intimate part and encourages the largest swan to nibble. Just then, 'That Man' appears. He is wearing an elaborate cape, strings of pearls and nothing else. He walks towards Bunty, visibly aroused, and tries to embrace her. The swans gather around her and noisily chase him away. Bunty continues her languorous shower, frequently touching her nipples and moaning. Meanwhile, he has fallen against hard rocks and is bleeding profusely. His eyes are shut. He could be dead. Bunty walks over to check, and kicks him in the ribs. He wakes up with a start and tries to pull her close. Bunty mounts him and instructs her swans to peck out his eyes. He screams in pain, but she doesn't want him to stop. She gets off him with a laugh ... and lets the hungry swans take over).

Two weeks later, while I was buying fruits on the narrow pavement opposite Breach Candy Club, his voice was near my ear, his breath close to my neck, as he said, 'Lychees, huh? Juicy juicy ... just like you. Hey you, K.K. ... want to be my kutti again? Drinks tonight? Yacht Club or Harbour Bar? I have rooms in both places ... the Taj beds are larger and more comfortable, Yacht Club prefers firm mattresses. You pick ...'

Not a word emerged from my mouth. I had taken in my breath and forgotten to exhale. His right hand was caressing my bare upper arm, while his left was attempting to interlink fingers with my free hand—the one not holding a bunch of lychees. 'I thought the swans had eaten you up ...' I stammered.

He laughed and ruffled my hair, 'Oh ... you call your hit men "swans"?' I whirled around, and right there in front of the fruitwalla, the bhuttawalla, the mochi and the bhelpuri man, apart from pedestrians jostling past us, I attached my wide open mouth to his and ate up his tongue. He nearly toppled over, which would have been a problem, since speeding cars with impatient drivers honking away, were whizzing past us.

'There are easier ways to kill me K.K. Death by snogging is not my style. So ... drinks tonight? I pick the Harbour Bar ... window table.' He sprinted across the road to a waiting Mercedes with tinted windows and got in. I was sure I spotted high heels in that flash when the car door opened. So, he was travelling with a woman in the opposite direction, heading to Bandra perhaps, or Juhu, where film people lived. I stared at the lychees and then at the fruitwalla.

'Thirty-five rupees Madam,' he said stonily. As if it was an everyday thing in his life for a customer to be ambushed. A female customer, quite familiar in the area at that, who thought nothing of being so besharam in public. Did full-full chumma. Did I care?

Suddenly, the lychees had acquired a magical power. Holding the bunch he had touched briefly with his fingers, made the lychees extraordinary. Armed with them, I was invincible. I danced all the way to the kitchen, twirled around, holding the lychees high up in the air!

'Lychees ... O ... lychees.' I sang. The Maharaj and his

assistants stopped slicing palak and bhindis and stared at me open-mouthed, then hastily looked away so as not to embarrass me. I rushed to my room to start hunting for the right 'look'. Saree? Why not? I looked my best in sarees. A flowered French chiffon, no bra, knotted choli, high heels, Miss Dior, Chanel bag, Patek Phillipe white gold watch with diamonds, pale lipstick … yes! Squirrel walked in just as I was leaving for the Taj.

His eyebrows shot up. 'Him?' I pinched his cheek and squeezed his butt playfully. 'Kushal has fever. Give him Paracetamol syrup. Khushboo needs new shoes. Byeeeeee.' He waved uncertainly. There was a worried look on his face.

He called out to me as I reached the porch and summoned the driver, 'So Srilaaji … Should I change the name of the Delhi house or not? Three Olives? Let me know.'

~

'You are such a loving kutti, yaar,' said 'That Man', and I melted. We were seated by the bay window, looking at the Gateway of India. The three olive martini was being sipped, as his fingers played with the starched serviettes.

'I hate that bitch. I am planning to kill her. I am serious,' I said, my chest heaving, my voice a hiss.

'Which one? I am surrounded by bitches …' he smiled indulgently.

'Stop smiling ... you are a total haraami. Worse than a kutta,' I snapped and knocked back a quick gin and tonic. 'He leaned across and licked my earlobe. 'Please yaar ... stop being a naagin. Your venom will not work on me. You were to show me some money, right? What happened? We had a deal.'

I looked away. As always, he had made it sound like it was all my fault. 'I tried ...' I replied defensively, 'But you disappeared ...'

He leaned back on the sofa and signaled for a fresh martini. 'I needed money then. Not five months later. Well ... I got it from some other bitch ... so, let's skip the excuses.'

Excuses? He dipped his index finger into the glass, held it up and said, 'Suck! You are good at it. The best. No better way to enjoy a martini ... keep sucking, K.K.'

The room in the heritage wing was beautiful. It overlooked the bobbing boats in the harbour and I could see the outlines of the islands close by. I removed my solitaire ear studs carefully and was taking off my bangles, when That Man lunged at me and started pulling off my chiffon saree a bit too roughly ... it was a crude, awful gesture. In the past I would've passed it for passion. But this time, the mood was different—very hostile and threatening.

I halted him by gripping his right wrist, 'Behave!' I reprimanded. He was taken aback and stared incredulously at me. Next second I felt the back of his hand across my right cheek—cracccck! It made a sharp sound, as I lost my balance and fell on the thick carpet. He pounced on my prone form and sat on my chest, pinning down my arms. I tried to thrash my legs to get out from under him, but his weight didn't let that happen. He placed one elbow across my chest, while the thumb of the hand that was free was pressed down on my wind pipe forcefully. I started to choke, but continued to move my legs. The pressure on my wind pipe was leading to a blackout, and my head was reeling. I gave up the struggle, and was ready for death. He loosened his grip and removed the thumb, leaving me to cough and gasp, cough and gasp.

He continued to sit on my chest, watching my face keenly. I guessed he had done this many times. With other kuttis. It was a first with me. Oh yes. It was easy to tell the brutality was practiced and perfected over the years. And all his kuttis had experienced it. Bunty included. I opened my eyes and saw him ... as if for the first time. 'That Man' was not a man at all. He was not even an animal. He was a shaitaan. I was the one that got away lightly, I thought to myself driving home. I could've been killed that night.

'Squirrel ... please let me in,' I said softly, so as not to wake up the household. It was 2:30 a.m. And I was feeling cold, feeling hungry, feeling ... feeling ... strangely alive! Squirrel moved over and made room for me on his bed—the same one he had slept on since his schooldays. 'Srilaaji ... you are home. Bas. You are home.'

I was alive. And I was home.

Before falling into deep sleep I told Squirrel, 'Two Olives, not three. The name of our Delhi home—just two. For us. For you and me ... good night.'

~

I gave up olives for life. And shunned martinis. Tuxedos made me laugh. But K.K. was harder to abandon. It suited me! I became K.K. without realising. And by the time I figured being K.K. was a full time 'job' with few rewards, it was too late. I still had zero friends. And I was still searching for Ma. At one point Ma became an obsession. I went back to Kolkata several times to try and put the pieces of her fractured life together. There weren't many people who had known her well. The bits I managed to excavate were scraps of no real value. She had very little real contact with the outside world.

I went to her old school and college (Loreto House), asked to meet her teachers, or get the contact numbers of friends she may have had back then. All the people I met talked about Ma in vague terms. They mentioned a 'sweet and simple girl' who hardly spoke. But I knew my Ma was not sweet nor was she simple. She was troubled. Did nobody figure that much out? Nobody? Not even Babuji! Or the shrewd and wise Buaji?

Getting to know Ma became a mission for a while. It led me to myself. And I wasn't impressed. Perhaps, like

Ma I was also running away ... but from whom? Why? My life was like the lives of so many other Marwari girls from a similar background. We were programmed and wound up to lead a particular kind of existence. Our choices were made for us at birth. We were told our future was predetermined. Our elders would decide the course of our lives, because they knew best. All we had to do was obey and conform. Not upset the family. Not bring shame to the community. If there was a problem that needed to be resolved, the community would handle it—not outsiders. Secrecy was everything. Our lips had to be sealed. Our emotions bottled. Our thoughts suppressed. We had to uphold the honour of the family we were married into, whatever the cost. Being a Marwari was a full time, ongoing exercise. It was as if there was the outside world of non-Marwaris and then there was us with our special world! With our specific codes, rules and regulations. Ma was different. I was her daughter. If Ma was troubled—what was I?

The old retainers clammed up when I went in search of answers. They feigned amnesia. They told me to forget the past ... to leave her memory alone.

'Why wake up the dead?' the retired, senior most driver asked me.

'I need to know!' I implored.

'No Babyji ... you don't need to know. There is nothing to know.' Blank, blank, blank. Squirrel was beginning to wonder about my frequent disappearances to Kolkata.

'Srilaaji ... you must relax your mind, na? Or else your health will suffer. If you want, we can move to Kolkata for a while. The children will be leaving for boarding schools soon. They won't miss us.' It was an offer worth taking ... but I didn't. Maybe I was tired of looking for Ma. Maybe, I didn't really want to know everything ... or even a little ... about this delicate beauty, a wisp of a woman, more an apparition than a human.

I tracked down her faithful maid, the one who was her shadow. Mishtidi was kind and tried to be helpful, but avoided answering direct questions. 'Where did Ma go every afternoon?' I asked. She smiled, 'To help poor people ...' That was it. No more information.

'What did she die of? Was she ailing?' Her eyes looked away and she offered to make me chai. 'Did my mother drink daaru? Was it alcohol that killed her?' She looked at her feet and shook her head. 'Why did she not tell anybody what was bothering her?'

She looked up, 'Tell whom? In your kind of families women don't tell anyone anything. They die with their secrets. They are not permitted to talk.'

I shot back, 'What nonsense! She could have told me! I was her child!'

'Children are always the last to know,' she said and in a way indicated our meeting was over. If it wasn't alcohol, what else could it have been? I spent hours in her old room, going through her things. Her French chiffons were still hanging in the large almirah ... her fragrance

(Guerlain) was everywhere. I sat on her bed—the bed she never ever invited me to share even as a little girl. There was a slight dent where her fragile body must have tossed and turned restlessly, night after night. I picked up her lace kerchiefs from the small drawer by her bedside. She must have shed unseen tears in them, I thought, as I kissed them one by one. I was afraid for myself on those trips. I didn't want my life to end like hers. I kept looking through her leather boxes with italicised initials stenciled on the side. One day, I would stumble upon that one clue, the key I was desperately seeking ... and then, I would finally find Ma, know Ma. Till then, I had to rid myself of memories that were incomplete and dissatisfying.

Squirrel suggested I see a hypnotist he was told had 'cured' many women. He added helpfully, 'Srilaaji ... those women are Marwari—like us—same community. It will make things easy.'

I wanted to laugh, instead, I found myself sobbing uncontrollably. This was not my life. I had to get out of the readymade Marwari mould if only to save myself. I was me! Much more than a typical Marwari woman. I turned to Squirrel and announced, 'I am ready!' Squirrel had the good sense not to ask, 'For what?' He hugged me tight and said, 'Let's eat some malai kulfi.'

PART THREE

WIDOW

Men still stared at my breasts. That was nice! Why lie? I hate it when women pretend they get offended when men look pointedly at their breasts. It is natural. Normal. Yes, women don't stare at men's crotches. Unless the men are wearing 'langots'. Then, of course, that is the only place the eyes go. Langots and ballet-dancer tights. Those, too. They conceal just enough to arouse our curiosity. Rather, forget curiosity—to arouse. I enjoy being aroused. It makes me feel wiggly and slightly giddy. Especially if I am in a car and there are many speed breakers on the road.

I had once asked a friend if she also felt the same, and she glared at me. 'You are a pervert ... you know that, Srilaa? A full pervert! Good, clean girls don't feel dirty things like that. We keep that part which is down there only for our husbands. Not for ourselves.' I ignored her. And in any case, she stopped talking to me. How stupid! So, even though, I was happy with my breasts and all that, I was not happy-happy. I was missing having a man in my life. A proper man. My precious solitaires were gone. 'That Man' had pocketed them neatly, after almost choking me to death. I realised I had left them in the hotel room. I started calling them my 'bad luck' solitaires. But they were a small price to pay for my freedom. I wasn't paralysed any more. I was breathing better. My voice was back. So was my appetite—for everything.

I looked at myself in the full length bathroom mirror—not bad! Well ... not perfect, either. Everyone in my circle was doing pilates, had personal trainers, went to the gym regularly, walked and swam. I did nothing. Men still talked to my chest, though. So, I felt fine! Here I was, hitting forty (actually, I had hit it long ago, but I always lied), and my breasts were holding up really nicely—not droopy at all. Even I talked to my breasts from time to time. They were sweet and comforting and I enjoyed staring at their different shapes, which altered according to my posture. I was not body obsessed, as such. But which woman is not vain? Despite feeling confident about myself on most levels, I still felt a lack of energy. I think it had to do with my diet. And an overall sense of non-fulfilment, which wasn't directly related to men and how they treated me. I hated my daily life and what appeared on the dining table. Even though Marwari kitchens had undergone a dramatic change, our meals were far too rich and oil soaked. I developed acidity and a bad temper.

One day, while I was arguing with a very grouchy Maharaj about the amount of oil he used in our everyday meals, an idea struck me—'Diet food for Marwaris'.

Especially for Marwaris. Sounded like a contradiction in terms, I know, but the Marwaris of my generation had also changed. They travelled the world and had become more health conscious. The women went to fancy spas and the men played golf. Everyone wanted to look 'fit and fine'. My idea was solid! If the Jains had their own food requirements, it was time for us to have ours. I spoke about it to Squirrel, who seemed genuinely excited and offered to propose it as a future business to the family. The concept was surprisingly well received, and Squirrel told me to go ahead and develop a business plan.

'Harvard,' I said flatly. Squirrel was puzzled, 'Meaning ... ?'

'I want to go to Harvard. That's the right way to go about it. People will respect me more if I am qualified. And I'll take advanced nutrition classes in Switzerland.'

Squirrel was not convinced and shook his head, 'Srilaaji ... what are you saying? It's too late to go back to studying ... soon our children will be applying to Harvard. Our time is over, na? We should concentrate on business, money, investment. When did you last touch a textbook? Forget Harvard-Shaarvard ... let's just go like that only to America, for fun.'

I grabbed his face roughly, looked deep into his eyes and snapped, 'I am going to Harvard, whether you like it or not. Whether you come with me or not. I will go in summer for six weeks. I have decided. It will be good for me. And good for business.'

Squirrel was blinking rapidly, 'But ... but ... Srilaaji ... what will I tell my family? And our friends?' I laughed, 'The truth, Squirrel. Just the truth. You will say, "Srilaaji wants to study business at Harvard ... she is going there in summer".'

Squirrel smiled, 'Srilaaji ... you toh, na? So smart you are! Why not? It's a great idea. Harvard will be fantastic! I am so proud of you! Let us both enroll ... I will also take the same course, we can attend the same classes. Eat ice cream, go skating ... achcha plan hai.'

Squirrel and I spent the best ten weeks of our entire married life that glorious summer in America. We had never experienced such joy in being together, doing simple, silly stuff, getting drunk in student bars, dancing in the snow, attending rock concerts, learning to ice skate in a rink, lying on the grass idly chatting, eating junk food non-stop. Bliss! I didn't want to go back to our Bombay life. To that mansion which never became my home. To my children, who didn't feel like my own. Squirrel may have felt the same way, but he staunchly and loyally defended his family, the awfully boring lifestyle we thought was luxurious but was in fact, steeped in poverty of the imagination, devoid of generosity on any level—emotional or financial. The charity work we underwrote was just a salve for our excess and waste. It meant nothing to us deep down.

'Charity work looks good,' I used to be reminded at family meetings. 'We should position ourselves as philanthropists. It brings respect and prestige to the group.' Away from such rubbishy conversations in America, I felt free to be myself. However bad I was. Or good—though, the 'good' option always eluded me.

And that's how 'Healthy Marwari' started. In the vacant family garage downstairs, which was converted into a packaging and dispatch centre, while I supervised one young maharaj who reported to Smita, a smart nutritionist I poached from the next door Jaslok Hospital. She understood food, calories, digestion, diets. And was an eager learner. We became friends pretty soon, even though she was fifteen years younger. But being single, she had all the time in the world to be around when I needed her.

We loved the new areas of the kitchen, which were generously given to me by Buaji. It was the old, unused pantry. The kitchen itself was planned by German experts and was space efficient. Our time at Harvard had brought Squirrel and me much closer, and we spent a lot of time giggling and chatting as we experimented with new foods and exchanged club gossip. The kids would run in and out, while other family members became our first guinea pigs and sportingly tasted every new product, filled forms, and gave ratings. I was getting a lot of respect now that I had demonstrated an entrepreneurial streak. I was introduced proudly as 'Our-Harvard-returned Bahu ...' which was embarrassing and untrue. I would mutter, 'No, no, no ... just a short summer course ...' But nobody really heard me.

The business grew beyond my expectations, and soon we were supplying 'Healthy Marwari' to stores across Bombay, and as far as Thane. One day Squirrel asked me, 'Srilaaji ... you can say "no" if you wish ... but our family wants to expand your business, invest in it, and make the brand national. They have already carried out a market survey. What do you think of the idea, Srilaaji?'

My hands were deep in a bowl filled with roasted nachni. I looked up, smiled sweetly and said, 'Tell them to fuck off!' Squirrel's face crumpled. 'Srilaaji ... I cannot say that, na?'

I replied, 'Say it in whichever language. But I mean it. This is my business. It will stay my business. Only mine. Now, get lost ... take the kids to the aquarium or to the club. I have work to do ... we are experimenting with oil-free papads. You can sample them next week—and fart less.'

I went in for foreign funding instead of depending on the family. I kept all the control. Of course. My German investors were impressed by my no-nonsense efficiency. One of them fell for the nutritionist and married her. Which was great—he shifted to Bombay. So I got two for the price of one! Hans and Smita became an invaluable part of my enterprise, after I opened a small factory, just outside Bombay. He sensibly quit his job and joined my company as the CEO. Our Marwari friends were very impressed and would tell each other, 'Just see her guts ... she has a firang CEO. Why can't we be like her?'

Naturally, every Marwari woman began to hate the sight of me. I had stopped wearing sarees and switched to tailored pantsuits. Like the ones I saw on power ladies, as they were called. Those who I imagined worked for Chase Manhattan Bank. The same ones featured in *Fortune* and *Businessweek*. I also cut my hair into a more practical bob and started wearing red lipstick. In social situations, I joined the men and enjoyed my whiskey. The women—especially the ones in stringy-backed cholis and organza sarees, glared at me and didn't bother to conceal their hostility. I heard from the notorious back biting gang, led by Mrs Jalan, that I was declared a negligent mother who never attended school events and only thought about making money and more money.

While saying all this, they were making more money for me, snacking on my 'Healthy Marwari' crunchies, and drinking sugar-free fruit juices from my brand. They'd go home feeling virtuous and then eat a ghee-soaked dal batti before heading off to snore. The irony was not lost on me—'Healthy Marwari' hahahaha!

I loved that ... and gloated in front of Squirrel, 'Seeeeeee—I've done it!' He grinned and squeezed my arm, 'I knew you were special, Srilaaji, from the moment you drew your vagina on the ground with a twig.'

I mock-scolded, 'Where does my vagina come into this? You can only think of sexual matters and my vagina! Really!' Squirrel's expression suddenly changed.

He looked momentarily lost and then said, 'No,

Srilaaji ... I can only think of Soumitro. All the time. Every moment ... I miss him very much. That is not to say I am insulting your vagina, Srilaaji ... but since you asked, I thought let me clarify.'

It was time to do something sweet for my sweet Squirrel. I asked the German to help.

Tracking down Soumitro with German expertise, was not as easy as I had imagined. It took Hans more than six months and a final trip to America to locate Soumitro in San Francisco. There was good news and bad. Soumitro was divorced. He was also jobless and broke. Excellent. I told Hans to get him back to India. To us. Soumitro said he wanted to speak to me first. Fair enough. Hans had told him Squirrel had zero idea about any of this. So, when I placed a call to Soumitro, he sounded guarded and cautious, as if suspecting a trap.

I put on my sweetest voice and spoke to him in lulling tones. Within minutes, he broke. His voice changed and he became a child looking for a saviour. He told me life was hard for him, especially after the divorce. He lived in different motels, taking up odd jobs. Often he didn't have enough to eat. He was slurring and I suspected he had a drinking problem—booze over food. Standard story. So long as it wasn't drugs, I could handle it. I had asked Hans to click pictures. Soumitro looked a wreck! He was a far cry from the polished, well-dressed, handsome Bengali gentleman with neatly parted thick hair. This person looked shabby and bedraggled ... a hobo. What if I paid so much money, did so much kharcha, brought him back especially for sweet Squirrel—and Squirrel rejected him? Then I'd be stuck with Soumitro. And there was no space in my life for a worthless hanger on.

I called back Soumitro after a few days and lots of thought. I spoke to him frankly and told him to stop sniffling. 'Firstly, I am not your mother. So, please stop crying. Your mess has been created by you. Who told you to leave my Squirrel, huh? How nicely we were looking after you! Such an ungrateful man—left my husband broken-hearted. Just like that. For no reason! Walked out of our lives! Ran off thousands of miles.'

Soumitro broke into Bengali. I said sharply, 'Look here, these calls are expensive, okay? I told you I am not your mother. Why are you speaking to me in Bengali? Forgotten English or what?'

He quickly switched and said limply, 'But ... but ... he had you. He had a proper family life. Children. Everything. I had nothing. On top it, everybody laughed at me! Called me all sorts of dirty names. I was a disgrace to my family. Ma and all the others shunned me. If I had not escaped then, I would have committed suicide.'

I said, 'But you didn't, na? You are alive. Talking nicely to me. Where is your family now? Idiot! Fool! Bloody gandu! Wake up! We are your family—Squirrel and I. We have money. If you come back, we will look after you. But before that, you will have to clean up your life. You must be having a Green Card, right? Come as a tourist, then we'll see.'

Squirrel was looking unwell, even though we had done all the tests at Breach Candy hospital and not found anything. He had started complaining of breathing problems. There was no asthma in his family. We had him checked for T.B., even lung cancer. Nothing showed. And yet, I would find him on the balcony coughing and gasping for breath. We consulted the top specialists, had X-rays done and tried various treatments from Ayurveda, homeopathy to the standard drugs. His weight was okay. He wasn't withering or anything. His appetite was good, and he slept well, except when he had breathing problems.

We were told it was the pollution in Bombay. Perhaps he suffered from an allergy to something in his immediate vicinity. Was it mites? We changed all the upholstery, his mattress and pillows, even the curtains in his room. Nothing helped. I started to monitor his diet closely, avoided nuts and lentils altogether; even stopped ordering fresh flowers in case pollen was the culprit. Nothing seemed to help my Squirrel. I felt miserable watching him straining to breathe. And I couldn't understand what was going wrong. Squirrel was not a smoker, his habits were clean and healthy. But clearly, he was suffering. And there wasn't much I could do to help him.

I suggested spending fifteen days at a hill station nearby—Mahableshwar. Maybe the relatively cleaner air there would get his lungs to breathe better. I engaged a highly-recommended yoga teacher to get Squirrel's breathing going right. The regular pranayam helped a bit initially, and then we were back to struggling again. I engaged a male night nurse to sleep just outside Squirrel's bedroom door. The first two or three were attentive and woke up when Squirrel coughed. The next few slept through everything. The children were told Squirrel was a little under the weather, but it wasn't a serious ailment. They were busy at school and the packed activity schedules at Sanawar ensured they didn't have time to brood. We saw them during the holidays—and that was more than enough.

I kept feeling I needed to demonstrate my love for Squirrel in some significant way. I was stuck and unsure what that gesture ought to be. I asked Smita one day when we were looking at spreadsheets. She turned to me and said, 'You do love him, don't you? Then why pretend?' I was startled out of my skin! 'Rubbish! What love? I don't know ... love has nothing to do with my wanting to be nice to a man I've been married to for so many years.' Smita wisely kept quiet.

Our wedding anniversary was coming up soon. One day before the date, a small box was delivered to my desk at the corporate office. It was a couriered package from Kolkata. I unwrapped it hastily and read 'B.C. Sen' on the maroon coloured box. My eyes brimmed over with tears when I opened it. Nestling on the satin lining of the box were two enameled gold pendants on delicate chains, surrounded by glittering diamonds—the pendants bore our wedding photograph. One pendant for me, one for Squirrel. Smita had ordered them that same day when we had discussed the peculiar nature of my love for Squirrel. I marveled at the thought and the execution. The enameling was just so beautiful ... I wore mine immediately. The pendant rested on my breasts so assuredly—like it knew it had found a home. I wanted Squirrel to wear his and rushed back from office ahead of time.

He was gone.

The family thought he was resting in the early evening, as he often did these days. They had told the staff not to disturb him. His driver was waiting to take him for an evening walk to the race course. His clothes were ironed and kept ready, along with his walking shoes. Even his tray was prepared in the kitchen, expecting the bell to ring, indicating he was up. The bell never rang.

He wore 'our' pendant on his last journey. He took me with him. And I never took mine off! Never.

The funeral was a sombre, grim affair. Most of the relatives were in shock at the suddenness of Squirrel's death. 'We had no idea he was so sick ... cancer? It's okay. Don't answer. Nobody likes to admit it.' It wasn't cancer. It was fibrosis, as the doctors confirmed subsequently. There is little that can be done to save someone struck by this dreaded condition. It is as if your lungs start shutting shop, gradually and stealthily, till one day the lungs declare a complete lock out. It can hit anybody at any age. It had hit Squirrel a bit too early.

The mourners whispered and mumbled. Some talked knowledgeably about a mysterious 'autoimmune disease' that was killing people like flies. Others kept mum, and squeezed my upper arms as they filed past the family, hands folded in a namastey, eyes lowered to show respect. Even in those sad moments, I noticed the sidelong glances of lecherous elders sizing me up—Squirrel's young and sexy widow was fresh meat in the market. I noticed my in-laws noticing. And then exchanging 'those' looks. The knowing kind which say, 'We always knew she was like that ... a loose woman of low character.' Maybe they were one hundred per cent right. I was in no hurry to prove them wrong.

Oh ... the children. Yes, they cried a bit. And were hugged and kissed by all. I spent time with Khusboo—she was at the age where she needed to establish her own territory. 'Mummy ... I need tranquillizers and sleeping pills. All my friends are telling me I need to pop something. I am stressed out, Mummy. Imagine, I had to cancel Akshita's dance practice suddenly! Her brother's sangeet is in Jaipur next week. My new Gudda lehenga will be wasted! I need those pills now! My dad has gone and died on us. This is terrible! What are we gonna do now, huh? Without pills, I will kill myself. If I die, so will Kushal. That will leave just you. Or, better plan—we can all take pills and die. Tonight sounds good. While all the aunties and uncles are still here for dad's funeral.'

I said not a word. I wanted to slap her hard. I should

have slapped her years ago—cheeky, ugly brat! Yes, ugly, too. Like my in-laws. Khusboo had inherited their worst features. But I wasn't feeling sorry for her at all. I said calmly, 'Beta, that's an idea worth thinking about. Thank you. I will check the correct dosage with the doctor. Please take a nap while I arrange for the pills. Bye!'

There were things to be done on priority. I called and gave Soumitro the news. He sounded annoyed. Like I had cheated him out of a free holiday to India. Smita and the German laughed when I told them how hurt I was after that call. Did Squirrel mean that little to him? I knew the answer, of course.

Then I asked them an important question: who else could I possibly have asked but Smita and the German? Going through Squirrel's things, I had found several love letters between him and Soumitro. Also many photographs of them naked and cuddling. Some close-ups of Soumitro's erections (oh—so THAT was the big attraction!) There were also photographs of Soumitro clad in my wedding saree. And Squirrel in a Bengali dhoti. How could I tell? Because Squirrel's erections were one-fourth the size. Right behind a stacked pile of Squirrel's imported underwear, I stumbled on several men's porno magazines and videotapes of male orgies, apart from packets of flavoured and textured condoms (definitely never used with me!).

There were also instructions to pay Soumitro

large sums of money. Carefully hidden under his monogrammed silk pajamas were bundles of cash, wrapped in newspapers. This was a contingency fund created for Soumitro in case Squirrel died in an accident or without making a will. Oh, the damn will! I looked hard for it. There was no will—and that made me really angry. I yelled at Squirrel, 'How could you do this? You've left me to sort out the mess!' I had taken to yelling at Dead Squirrel pretty regularly. Something I rarely resorted to when he was alive. All those years of not shouting and screaming at the kindest and most loving human being in my life, were making me nervous. Why didn't I protest earlier? Why did I keep quiet? It's not as if he didn't anger me. I wanted to make up for it now that he wasn't there to hear my cries of rage. It was my way of telling Squirrel I loved him.

'Burn everything!' Smita said flatly. 'What? Burn such precious stuff?' Smita turned to the German and said, 'Hans ... you explain.' So the German explained.

In a businesslike tone and minus any sentimentality. 'Only you know about all these things your husband left behind—yes?'

'Yes.'

'If you burn it all, nobody will miss it, yes?'

'Yes.'

'You don't want to keep naked pictures of your husband and his lover—yes?'

'Yes'.

'You want to keep the cash—yes?'

'Yes'.

The matter was settled.

I took the cash and made diamond bangles for Khushboo and diamond achkan buttons for Kushal. The rest was spent on buying gold coins for my future grandchildren. I believed in the power of gold—the only inflation-proof product in the world. And investing in blue chip stocks for myself. I left a little something in my personal locker—for emergencies. Most women are very gullible, trusting and foolish. They also think emergencies happen to other people. Not me. I was a Marwari—'by khoon'—as Squirrel used to tease me. 'Khoon' counts for a lot in our community. We don't accept outsiders and half-breeds easily. If I wanted hard cash in a hurry—I now had it! And nobody could take it away. Nobody knew it was with me! Thank You, Dead Squirrel. Soumitro's loss was my gain. Divine justice. We were quits.

~

I decided to change the name of our Delhi bungalow (it was all mine, now). My first option was 'Olive'. On second thoughts (always the best ones), I decided on 'One Olive', as a funny cosmic hat tip to Dead Squirrel. It sounded more poetic. The new polished brass plaque was installed on Valentine's Day. I cried a little. Then made myself a sharp martini. With one olive. The first martini after I had sworn I wouldn't go near one after 'That Man's' betrayal. It was done—closure. All it took was a game played with a Mediterranean fruit. No more extra olives in my life from that point on.

PART FOUR

'SADHVI'

Thus began my new life as a Marwari widow.

A whip in one hand, and a cheque book in the other.

I was single, wealthy, successful, powerful and desirable.

But what was I supposed to do with my desire? Now, more than ever, I wanted sex. Proper, regular sex. Not sneaky sex in hotel suites. Not guilty sex in some strange city. I wanted healthy sex to go with my 'Healthy Marwari' brand! With a regular man at regular intervals in regular settings. Masturbation was not for me. I was far too lazy to think of ways of achieving an orgasm without a partner—man or woman. I used to try and stimulate my libido (a lovely word Smita introduced me to!) by looking at adult men's magazines (had kept a few from Dead Squirrel's collection), but I would feel like giggling—all those men with unusually large penises of odd shapes and at crooked angles did not excite me at all.

I wanted a man whose hard-on I could see through his pants. Whose breath was a mix of peaty whiskey and a good cigar, whose nipples hardened just like mine when we were together, whose armpits were fresh-smelling—I had a weakness for Davidoff's Cool Water. I liked my man to have muscular calves and strong thighs. Hairless shoulders and a powerful neck. I was not put off by a slight paunch (I had one myself). But the man's butt had to deliver on my erotic scale. Mine was ample and juicy. I didn't like hairy, smelly navels, but that was a minor issue and easy to fix. What was much tougher was to get rid of the 'hing' odour that emerged in sweat. A hing embrace was the worst put-off. Most Marwari men sweated hing from every pore.

What else? I was a sucker for some atmosphere. An ambience (another word I heard Smita use often!) that was conducive to love making. Hard, quick sex was fine too ... but only if I had the softer version first. I mentioned all this to Smita and the German. They didn't laugh at me. Instead, they listened attentively and concluded I wasn't looking for just a regular fuck—I was looking for a sensitive lover. Smita, in her pragmatic way, told me bluntly, 'Such men don't really exist. You get husbands. And then you get professional fuckers. But who knows? Are you ready to seduce? Seduction takes time, patience, cunning, strategy, luck. Can you wait that long?'

No. I couldn't. Sorry.

My business was going fine. I was being feted and celebrated by all the Marwari-run organisations for women. I was invited to colleges and schools to share my success story. I opened art shows and cut ribbons at trade shows. Financial papers ran flattering profiles of how I had done it. I was seen as a patron of the arts, with promising painters lining up to gift me their works so that they could list me as a collector in their next catalogue. But I was missing K.K.—the asli kutti. And before my necklines plunged any lower in a pathetic bid to tell the world I was still in the game, I decided to consult an influential punditji.

My plan was simple. I invited him over and offered him warm milk with honey and freshly ground turmeric. He thought I was looking for an alliance for my 'kanya'—Khushboo. I said, of course, but she is only a teenager. He told me, the search for eligible grooms in the Marwari community starts early ... very early. He had a list of high school and college-going boys if I wanted to glance at it.

I came to the point quickly. 'Punditji ... The person I am looking for is not for my kanya, but myself!' He gulped. And paused before recovering his studied punditji mannerisms. With an exaggerated courtesy he said smoothly, 'I see ... I see ... I see.'

I corrected him, 'No Punditji, I don't think you have understood. I am not looking for a rishta. I am not interested in re-marriage. I am looking for a steady companion from a good, respectable background.' There was a long silence. He opened his almanac and consulted the stars. He asked for my birth date and exact time of birth. Before he left, after taking a hefty fee for his time, he answered slowly and carefully, 'I think I might have the right match for you, Bhabhiji ... give me a week.'

Punditji phoned three days later. He wanted to meet me urgently, he said, but not at my home. 'I don't trust servants. They are the biggest spies. Servants, drivers, dhobis and barbers—all are rascals. Walls have ears, Bhabhiji ... you never know who is listening. These days, family members place those recording things in each other's rooms, even in bathrooms. Better to meet outside, under the open sky, but not under any tree. Maybe seaside is best. Okay ... come to Worli Sea Face. I know a spot there.'

~

'Bhabhiji ... in your case, there is a big problem. I can find the men, but where will they meet you for ... for ... romancing? Your pictures come in the papers, people in our samaj know you well, you are highly respected, you do all that charity-warity, that becomes a handicap. Men feel scared of ladies like you, Bhabhiji, I am being frank.'

I glared at him, 'You called me all this way, to sit on a rough stone bench, in the presence of hundreds of people, to tell me this? As if it is something I have not thought about. Let's not waste each other's time—namastey. Here's money for your taxi fare.' Punditji was sweating profusely. He wanted to eat ice cream from a vendor before leaving. I paid for a cone.

He pleaded, 'Bhabhiji ... don't get me wrong. You are misunderstanding what I am saying. I am just telling you there are special challenges for ladies in your bracket—hi-fi ladies. You are not an ordinary Marwari widow—dukhi and miserable. You are a known lady. A lady with wants! I know men who are willing to fulfill your wants. But we have to find the right place for such meetings.'

I found the place I was looking for. It took me a month of research. But I found it! Without Punditji's interference. I didn't need Punditji's help ever again.

~

'My name's Allwin Coutinho, ma'am. But mostly, the locals know me as Alley Cat. How can I help you, Ma'am?' I had landed in Goa two hours earlier. The local real estate agent had ditched me. I was standing stupidly in the middle of nowhere, staring at a paddy field on one side, and a half-finished building on the other. 'Am I in Arpora? Is this the place?'

The man smiled, 'Yes, ma'am ... you are in Arpora. Who are you looking for? It is a small village. We all know each other.'

I fished out a shabby business card, 'This man.'

Alley Cat threw back his head and laughed, 'Oh, that no-good fellow? Cardoz? He's my cousin's boyfriend. I think they are doing some masti over there ... afternoon, no? We Goans like a little masti before our siesta. But maybe I can help you, ma'am?'

I was fuming. I knew I should have brought the

German with me on this trip. What did I know about the Goan ways of doing deals? I was looking for a space to start a 'Healthy Marwari' outlet in Goa. Someone had suggested Cardoz's name saying he was the sharpest real estate agent in Goa and I would conclude my deal within three days. If this was 'sharp' ... but my time was limited so I turned to Alley Cat, and in an exasperated tone I asked him if he could fill in for his cousin's boyfriend. Wrongly worded, I admit.

'Fill in? For what exactly, ma'am? You also want a little masti?' I wanted to box this insolent man in tight frayed jeans.

'Who are you?' I asked in my hoity-toity voice, reserved for servies and underlings.

'A lazy Goan, ma'am. And you? From Bombay! I can tell you people. All Bombaywallas talk like you ...' and then he mimicked me! Cheeky bloody bugger.

I turned to walk away, but he grabbed me by the shoulder, 'Just fooling, ma'am ... come on, let's get some feni.'

It was like every Goan cliché had come together like in a Bollywood script. Lazy Goan bugger called Alley Cat, a missing Goan real estate agent bonking his girlfriend instead of attending to work, the feni offer ... paddy fields, pigs, a whitewashed church in the distance. I was feeling giddy, but in a nice way. I turned down the feni offer and asked the ruffian if he knew a decent place for rent.

'How long?'

I thought quickly and said, 'One month.'

Even though I had planned to be away for just a week. Nobody would give me a good place for a week. And I was willing to pay upfront for a month (Thank you, Dead Squirrel! God bless you ... hope you are having fun in heaven). The crazy man grabbed my shoulder again and said, 'Come on ... I'll get my bike.'

And off we went down an uneven dirt track, with me hanging on to this crazy fellow's shoulders. He was singing to himself, and I wondered whether he was going to stop at a secluded spot and try being inappropriate with me. No. Worse than that—rob me! I had heard horror stories about these Goan ruffians preying on well-heeled single women.

Ten minutes later, we stopped at a villa with a charming name: Rosa Maria. He informed me grandly, 'My aunt's place ... she only rents to posh people like you. Bombaywallas. And foreigners. No Dilli people. She finds them rude and crude. Come in, ma'am. She has five cats and one dog. She talks a lot. But cooks well. You will like it here.'

I liked him. But didn't reveal a thing. I looked disinterested and distant, as three cats jumped from the balcony and started rubbing themselves against my leg. 'See ... the cats like you. Even I like you, ma'am ...'

I blushed and almost simpered, much to my embarrassment. 'Please stop this nonsense. I want to meet your aunt first and then decide. I have a booking at the Taj Aguada in any case.'

He smiled, 'I am very impressed, ma'am. Very nice hotel for very rich people. My uncle is a chef there. Two cousins work as waiters in the beach restaurant. I will tell them to give you extra portions. I also have an uncle looking after room service, and an aunt who heads housekeeping. You go there after meeting my aunt. I will introduce you to everyone.'

'Thanks a lot,' I said stiffly, adding in a silly aside, 'All the Taj people know me well ... I am well taken care of.'

He threw back his head full of unruly curls and laughed uproariously, 'Come and eat my auntie's marble cake and then talk, ma'am!'

I wagged a finger in his face, 'Stop this ma'am-ma'am nonsense. I know you are making fun of me!' He held my hand and led me to Rosa Maria's cool and cheerful salon, filled with graceful rosewood furniture.

'Portuguese. Belonged to my great grandfather. We call ourselves Portuguese. In our family, we speak to one another in Portuguese, not Konkani. One should always respect ancestry—do you agree?' I remained non-committal and tried to look unimpressed, even though I was staring wide-eyed at all the beautiful old oil lamps and an exquisite gilded altar. I was so engrossed, I didn't notice the petite form of Rosa Maria slipping silently into the salon, from her private quarters at the back of the villa.

'Welcome, dear ...' she said politely, holding out her tiny hand. She was dressed in what is called a 'house frock', with delicate lace at the neck and on the sleeves. No lipstick. No make-up. But eyes like pale emeralds, shiny and alert. Her hair was neatly pinned at the nape with mother-of-pearl combs. On a thin gold chain she wore an elaborate pendant with Mother Mary and Baby Jesus enameled on it.

She saw me looking and said, 'My mother's ... and before that, her mother's.'

She indicated it was time for tea by ringing a tiny silver bell on a side table, covered with a crotchet cloth. 'As a young Portuguese girl, in our village, it was compulsory to learn these arts.' Alley Cat was smiling, and idly picking up photo frames placed on the mantle. He had become Alley Cat inside my head by now.

He looked up, caught my eye and winked. 'Eat some cake—auntie is famous in our village for her cakes. Lemon sponge with icing, my favourite.'

Rosa Maria turned to me and asked, 'Is this rascal fooling you? Don't believe a word of what he says.' It was clear she adored him.

Her emerald eyes were shining as she urged me to tuck in. 'Show the lady around our estate,' she instructed Alley Cat, and he gallantly held out his arm. 'I can manage,' I was suddenly self-conscious.

Done. I was in. And perhaps done for, too.

Five days of hanging around waiting for the agent to show up, was telling on me. Even though, I had succumbed to the Goan tempo, where nothing much happened, but everybody looked happy. I still hadn't tasted feni. And Alley Cat had disappeared. Auntie kept to her part of the cavernous bungalow, while her staff looked after me. The food varied, from local to what we call 'continental'. Bombay was not on my mind. Nor was Delhi.

I was painting my toenails, a faded caftan riding way above my knees when a voice said, 'Here ... let me do that ... I am very good at it. Used to work as a pedicurist in a fancy salon in Panjim for fancy ladies like you.' I was startled. Then angry. Angry that he had left me alone for five days. His nonchalance and easy ways were annoying me.

'I need to get back if I can't find a good location for my store,' I said exasperatedly. He held up his hand and made a call, speaking in a mix of Konkani and Portuguese, with plenty of English swear words thrown in. 'Shut your ears, madam,' he said, while continuing the conversation. Ass! Little did he know—my repertoire of gaalis would have shamed him into embarrassment. Especially my colloquial Bengali ones! One day Alley Cat would be at the receiving end of my choicest.

It was done. I got my store. And I acquired a boyfriend. The rogue I had dismissed as a no good, beach bum, turned out to be a failed architect and prominent landlord with impressive holdings, paddy fields, cashew and coconut plantations, old homes in and around his ancestral village, a few commercial buildings in Panjim, two trendy restaurants with foreign chefs, a stake in the football team ... and wait—he also had his own band.

He played the saxophone, sang off-key mandos when drunk, and preferred his battered up motorbike to the fancy Merc in his garage. Our first night together was quite hilarious. To begin with, I caught him peeing in Rosa Maria's garden.

I startled him by shouting, 'Not on the roses! Please! They hate uric acid.' He tried to pull up his zip ... and I heard him cuss. That's when I discovered Alley Cat's aversion to underwear.

I was laughing as I went up to him and said, 'Why did you stop? Please finish the job? You think I have never seen men pee? Besides I want to watch you as you pee. I have a theory about men and their peeing habits.'

He refused. I was most disappointed. I walked back to the house. And he walked towards his bike. He was leaving. I was devastated. Maybe I would never see him again.

I shouted, 'There is freshly made lemon cake—I saved a slice for you.' He looked over his shoulder, paused and waved. Why the wave? Goodbye?

'I need to wash my fingers ...' he muttered as he walked past me and went into my bedroom. I was so relieved to see him this close to me, I was ready to dance with joy, but kept my head low, and followed him. My room was a mess. Two bras were dangling from the back of the chair, a discarded pair of discoloured panties was on the bathroom floor—not my pretty ones, but the lousy, out of shape everyday ones. My handbag was wide open and thrown on the bed, there was jewellery strewn on the dressing table, and the sandy chappals which I had kicked off after a walk on the beach had created a trail of seaweed stuck on the soles.

The bed was rumpled and unmade, a freshly ironed cotton salwar-kameez was placed on the pillow by Mary, the maid. But at least the room smelled fragrant, and the toilet was clean. I was near the writing desk waiting for him to emerge from the bathroom.

He came out grinning, 'I thought you wanted to watch me pee ... I took my time expecting you to walk in ... then I couldn't hold it in. Where's the bloody cake?'

We had the cake after.

Sex makes one so hungry. And I had been starving for weeks. Alley Cat was not a skilled lover. But he was considerate. He waited. And best of all, he didn't talk during sex. None of that rubbish stuff silly men imagine women get turned on by. He wasn't clinical or anything. Just efficient and attentive, using the right amount of pressure on the right spots at the appropriate time. I was dry and tight and self-conscious—it had been a while, after all. He moistened me with his saliva and I thanked him in a formal voice! He smiled and replied equally formally, 'You are welcome, ma'am.'

Later, I told him not to call me ma'am. He kept quiet, ate his lemon cake, picked up his bike keys and softly said, 'Good night, ma'am.'

Ma'am stayed. And so did he. I called him 'AC'—

short for Alley Cat. And over the next few months, we developed a calming, soothing relationship, which suited us both. I was not too interested in his life on an everyday basis. And he wasn't particularly curious about mine. I divided my time between Bombay and Goa, and was pleasantly surprised to see the response to 'Healthy Marwari'.

Srilaaji's Fantasy

AC and I are at a Goan wedding being conducted by a handsome, young parish priest. The bride and groom look like they belong on top of a three-tiered cake. There are about a hundred people inside the beautiful, whitewashed church. I can see Ma in one of the pews. She is fanning herself elegantly, and smiling at everyone. Her fan is made out of pale pink ostrich feathers. She turns around and waves when she spots me and AC. We join her and listen keenly as the wedding vows are taken. Once outside the church premises, I ask AC to dance, even though nobody else is dancing. He laughs and pulls out two blindfolds. 'Let's try a new step,' he says. Ma encourages both of us and helps tie the blindfolds. I can hear a band strike up a tango. I can also hear Squirrel's voice as he tells Ma, 'Your daughter Srilaaji is like a wild cat ... ' Ma's tinkling laughter is in sync with the beats of the tango. I cling on to AC. But he is no longer AC. Rather, his clothes have changed. I run my hands up and down his body. His fragrance has changed as well. I want to tear off the blindfold—could

I be in the arms of the parish priest? That definitely felt like a freshly laundered cassock under my adventurous fingers! I love the way I am being cradled and held. 'La Comparasita' is about to end. I call out to AC and tell him to play another tango. I feel Dead Squirrel's breath near my ear as he whispers, 'I like the priest, too! A lot!' Ma's laughter is echoing in my ears. I push the blindfold up from my eyes. Ma is slow-dancing with AC ... they look very happy together. She is wearing just her trademark lace lingerie, and AC is naked, waist down. His shirt buttons are open, and he has kept his shoes on. Ma is wearing pale blue kitten heels. Her hair is side swept and held together with a tortoise shell clip. I sigh. This is how it was meant to be.

It wasn't just Marwaris on a diet buying out our well-packaged snacks, but a lot of hippies and firangs. Smita and the German were very pleased about the business growing. But I had kept AC a secret from them. I didn't know how to 'explain' him—even to myself. I was not in love with him. He was not in love with me. Clear. But both of us chose to spend time together whenever possible. And we made 'possible' happen a lot! I did not question him, and he did not question me.

After some time, we were accepted as a couple, and I was called 'that Marwari woman' by locals. Some referred to me as 'Coutinho's gf'. I was indifferent. Goa had started to grow on me. There were lots of bfs and gfs floating around. I met them at Sunday mass in the village, which I used to enjoy attending with AC. The parish priest loved him and told me about his baptism feast, which the entire parish still spoke about.

AC used to dress carefully for church and wear a rakish hat, which always made me laugh. I was experimenting with my clothes as well, and wearing 'frocks' (it took me a while to figure out how to present my exposed legs to curious eyes). On a trip to Bombay, I asked Smita and the German to take me shopping.

'I need wraparound skirts and shorts,' I said somewhat sheepishly. They looked at one another and the German wiggled his eyebrows but kept quiet. Smita took me to her friend's boutique, and I excitedly bought what I called my 'Goan wardrobe'. It was time to confess.

'I have met a man ...' I started and Smita burst out laughing.

The German raised his eyebrows quizzically, 'Are you moving to Goa permanently?'

'No! Why would I do that?'

Smita answered quickly, 'For love?' Why lie? A little bit of love was happening. It was a nice feeling. Dead Squirrel would have been happy to see me like this.

I answered carefully, 'Not love-love exactly, but he's a good man. Come to Goa and meet him.' Two weeks later, they showed up, and met AC at the airport. When we picked them up, I said casually, 'This is AC. He is cooking dinner for us tonight.'

The German liked AC, Smita was less enthusiastic.

'What is all that ma'am-ma'am nonsense? He is okay. But not your type,' she pronounced dismissively later, when we were alone.

I had asked defensively, 'What is "my type" and how would you know, anyway?' She was stumped. And backed off.

The German smiled a lot, winked and said, 'Ignore my wife. I think she's jealous. Your boyfriend is handsome and smart'. Ha! Like I needed a certificate from him. Boyfriend! What a cheap and immature word! As if to put my relationship in place and dismiss it like some trivial fling I was idiotic enough to enjoy. I would prove them wrong. AC was the right man for me. I didn't care a damn what these two thought. With AC I had discovered my own passions, and not just for adventurous sex. My life in Goa was filled with sweet moments—as sweet as the lemon cake AC loved. What would these two know about simple pleasures? Had they ever been naked on the beach and danced under the stars? Had they let the sun enter their most intimate parts, while gentle waves tickled their toes as they waited for the tide to come in? No chance! So shut up, donkeys!

The dinner went off reasonably well. AC had taken the trouble to cook himself in the kitchen of his beach restaurant. He didn't do that too often, not even for visiting celebrities and rock stars. He had done it for me. Yes, me. Not those two. Close to midnight, the three of us decided to come back to Rosa Maria's villa for a beer, after AC roared off on his bike and headed to one of his 'town' homes, as flats in Panjim were called. Smita looked around my room and exclaimed, 'I can't believe you are living like this! Even your maids in Bombay have larger rooms.' Smita didn't get it. It wasn't about space. Or maybe she was a little jealous? The German approved and said he liked every inch of that room since it was 'charming' and 'authentic'. I looked at him gratefully and mouthed a 'thank you'.

The business was doing well. And I had thought of taking it to Kolkata. Smita was not that keen, but the German sounded enthusiastic. I had plans to set up an Arts' Foundation in Goa, which would keep me connected to what had established itself so well in Delhi. We could hold art camps and undertake community projects—AC had approved when I had brought it up with him, late one afternoon, just after making love. I mentioned AC's reaction enthusiastically, making it clear that his approval mattered to me. Smita snorted derisively and said, 'Let's just call it a love project. Forget you are a businesswoman. This makes no sense.' It was late and I was feeling genuinely hurt. The German squeezed my shoulder affectionately before leaving. Smita was wrong. It was much more than a silly little love project. I would prove it.

~

AC remained incommunicado for the next few days. It was a part of a pattern I had accepted. After a few hours of intimacy and closeness, AC would disappear without an explanation. I had taught myself not to brood during these absences. I would wait. And mope. Talk to pigeons. Giggle with Dead Squirrel. But keep mum. No questions asked when he'd show up later, like it was perfectly okay to abandon me. Despite these disruptions, I was turning into a Goan gradually. My days and nights would glide by at a languorous pace. I ate well. Drank a lot. Slept better.

I used to go back to Bombay most reluctantly. The gaps had become longer and longer. There was always an excuse to stay back, always something that needed my presence in Goa. Staying in that grand mansion, surrounded by servants and in-laws I had nothing left to share with, had created a stifling environment which was getting to me. I liked feeling the sand between my toes as I walked barefoot on my favourite beach. I now had a scooter in Goa and I loved to go to the neighbouring villages to buy fruits and fresh vegetables. The weekly market at Mapusa was always a surprise, especially if AC and I went together and chatted with the farmers. The small artists' community had accepted me and we were always invited to join their friends for an impromptu meal. I had started eating crab, mussels, clams, even pork. AC would bring freshly baked pie and we would sit at a shack drinking beer, sometimes chatting, sometimes not. Just being ourselves and feeling comforted.

That comfort zone was about to be shattered.

And it was Khusboo who wrecked it, by turning up unannounced in Goa.

'What are you doing here?' I asked in horror. Our relationship over the years had slid from polite affection to aloof resignation and more recently to distinct hostility—mainly from Khusboo's side. Thank God we didn't look alike! She was more Dead Squirrel than me.

Here she was, standing outside, in the patio of what I considered 'my' little home, and looking entirely ridiculous in her very fancy city clothes, high heeled pumps, a vulgarly expensive snake's skin bag and large, glittering diamond bracelets on both her wrists, multiple rings, a solitaire choker around her throat, and faux stones even on the buckle of her leather belt. I noticed my old Cartier watch and smiled. She did not smile back.

'Where is he?' she snarled.

'Who?' I asked.

'Oh please, mother ... stop acting like Virgin Mary. Where is your Goan lover? The one who is out to cheat not just you, but all of us?' What was she saying? 'I am planning to file criminal charges ... by the way. You may be a big, fat fool. But he cannot fool me. Smita has told me everything. I have proof.' Khushboo was out of control, yelling and screaming hysterically. The cats showed up. The pigs started grunting. Crows flew off the trees. A couple of coconuts fell to the ground, village dogs barked ... and just as I was about to slap this woman who was my daughter, a quiet voice said, 'Do come in ... have some almond cake and tea. You must be tired.' It was the gracious lady of the manor herself—tiny, dignified, proud.

~

I thought of Ma. At that very moment, I felt Ma was standing next to me and saying, 'Sweetie ... ignore this silly outburst. Daughters can be so annoying.' Really! What did Khushboo think? That I would shrivel and quake and fall apart because of her wild and baseless allegations? With Ma and Dona Rosa Maria by my side, I felt emboldened enough to walk up to Khushboo and give her a tight slap. The one I should have given long ago. Suddenly, I realised I had not touched my daughter in years. This unexpected physical contact was alien and I recoiled, as if my hand had fallen on an exposed electric wire.

Khushboo looked equally startled and was about to lunge at me, when Dona Rosa Maria nimbly stepped between us and held Khusboo by the shoulders, 'Calm down, child ...' she said gently. I thought I heard Ma's tinkling laugh—I loved her laugh. I was certain she was in the room with us. I could smell her fragrance. I felt a tap on my shoulder. Of course, it was Ma. It had to be Ma. I had nothing to fear. Khushboo was behaving like an idiot, making an utter fool of herself. I would deal with

Smita later. I turned to thank Ma. She was gone. By now, I had accepted what had happened to her fragile lungs. I desperately wanted to know what had destroyed her fragile mind. Would I also go the same way?

It was time to take out my whip and get into hunterwali mode. Khushboo deserved no better. Brat. Bitch. I blew Ma a kiss. A wispy swathe of French chiffon touched my bare, tanned Goan shoulder. I realised I had become a Marwari Goan.

~

AC was hardly shocked to see me when I determinedly rode my scooter to his Panjim office. I was wearing shorts. My hair was tied in a bandana with a skull pattern on it. One of those impulsive Night Market buys from a Rasta musician. My tee was fitted and said, 'Oranges and lemons sold for a penny.' AC was in denims, sandals, linen shirt. He was smoking. And hadn't shaved for a week.

'Khushboo landed up and screamed her head off ...' I blabbered.

He coolly asked, 'Who's Khushboo?'

Oh! How stupid of me. How would he know? We didn't discuss family. Maybe he knew I had grown-up children—a girl and a boy—maybe not. I must have looked comical at that moment. But AC did not laugh. He came towards me and held out his arms. I also asked myself, 'Who's Khushboo?' Blank.

AC suggested a beer and a joint—I jumped at the offer. I was not a pothead. Not yet. But I liked what I felt after a few deep drags. Besides, despite my feigned indifference, Khushboo's sudden arrival had rattled me enormously. She had screamed, 'Selfish bitch!' several times, her face inches away from mine. She had accused me of being a negligent, irresponsible, cruel mother. She had repeatedly said I was a 'sex-starved hag', a 'common whore' and a 'man-eater'. She also accused me of stealing her inheritance and cheating her. Such hatred! Such truth! I wanted to sit on the beach and talk to Dead Squirrel—I did that a lot. But Dead Squirrel must have been busy and I was left with AC. I decided to make a sand castle and tell him a little about my life before him. Just a little. I used shells and pebbles to create the family tree. The prettiest shell was Ma. And the least attractive pebble was me.

~

It was time to go back to Bombay and my other life. The one I desperately wanted to leave behind. Khushboo had flounced off in a huff, refusing Dona Rosa Maria's gracious offer to stay the night. I was dreading meeting Smita, now that Khushboo had implicated her. But there was no way I could postpone the inevitable—fire them both. Yes, the German, too. Regardless. It had been my error of judgment in allowing so much intimacy, such proximity. My need for them was over. I'd be fine without them. And they'd be whatever without me—did I care? My Buaji's words came back to me. 'It's best to trust our own people. They understand our ways. Outsiders remain outsiders, no matter what you do. They want more and more and more. Marwaris are better off with other Marwaris.' She was right.

The sacking was swift and clinical. I did not give Smita the chance she must have hoped for—to lecture me on my failings. I knew what I wanted. I knew what I was doing. She and the German had no place in my future plans. Both were replaced by Babuji's trusted men. I had known them since I was a child and that connection was enough. 'Healthy Marwari' was growing and it was their suggestion to induct Kushal into the business. After all, it would be his one day. Kushal was interested but not terribly bright. He liked his cars and golf and preferred to spend his time with a group of Boston friends. He resented the old style of doing business, and wanted to be treated like a boss. His immaturity annoyed me, but I also needed an ally. Kushal was weak enough not to challenge my authority. And I was devilish enough to pander to his ego. With a huge office and a pliant staff, Kushal felt important and secure. He started strutting around and behaving like a typical Marwari Seth ka bachcha. Sweet Dead Squirrel was never like that.

I had to create something for Khusbhoo to do—at least on paper. One morning, as I was dreaming of Goa, and longing for AC's breath on the back of my neck, I remembered Ma had a name. A lovely name. Sreemoyee. Nobody ever called her that. Nobody ever called her anything. Babuji's men were going through some files in my office when they came across Ma's and Babuji's marriage certificate, and wedding pictures.

'Sreemoyee Bhabhiji looks so beautiful here ...' they said showing me the photograph. That's when I remembered. We found some more pics—Ma looking so relaxed and happy, posing in front of a Swiss chalet.

'Honeymoon pictures ...' exclaimed the men. Then out fell a set of Ma and Babuji ballroom dancing at the Savoy in London. She was wearing a mink shrug over a chiffon saree, her hair up in curls, eyes shining brightly. One of the men made a clicking sound with his tongue before muttering, 'This was their last holiday together ... before Bhabhiji fell sick.' They shook their heads and looked embarrassed. I waited a bit before asking, 'How did Ma fall sick? What happened?' They exchanged looks, shuffled their feet and folded their hands, 'Madamji ... better you ask someone from the family. We don't know ...' I shut the door firmly and turned to face them, 'I want to know.'

Ma's story was sad. I knew it would be sad. But not this sad. The two men stuttered and stammered through the narration, insisting what they were revealing was mere hearsay ... but ... 'Sreemoyee Bhabhiji's parents had not told Babuji's family the truth when the proposal was sent. They had kept many things hidden from him. Bhabhji was not normal ... she had a mental problem. Just like her maternal aunt. The one nobody was allowed to meet. Bhabhiji was taking very strong drugs, to keep herself under control. Only her doctors knew what to give her. Without those medicines, Bhabhiji would become a different person ... hitting, biting, scratching and shouting. Nobody could control her then. Babuji found out soon after they came back to Kolkata after enjoying their honeymoon in Europe and England. Her parents were called over and asked for an explanation. By then it was too late—Bhabhiji was already pregnant.' That explained me! Somewhat. A product of a honeymoon celebrated by a groom who didn't know his bride was mentally ill, and a bride who had no idea her groom would be too shocked to take care of her when he found out.

That same night, I slept very well. I called AC and told him I was not coming back to Goa. He said, 'Okay ma'am. Good night.' That settled it. No fuss. No explanations. No guilt.

Dead Squirrel was more understanding. It was a monologue, of course. But I knew he was listening carefully. I tried to reach Ma. But Ma was Ma. She would find me when she wanted to, not when I needed her. I woke up fresh and strong at 4:30 a.m. and wrote out my plan to start the Sreemoyee Foundation for Mental Wellness. I would entrust it to Khushboo. I could see a bit of Ma emerging in her, and the role I had in mind for my troubled and anxious daughter, would, in due course, help her to get better, feel better. It would help me, too. I needed help ... more than Ma ... more than Khushboo. I needed to know me.

Srilaaji's Fantasy

AC walks up to me as I lie on a shabby deckchair. The beach is crowded this afternoon. Tourist buses with eager gawkers and voyeurs, rush to see naked people sunbathing on the sand or frolicking in the sea. The tide is coming in. I can hear the delighted screams of unruly children as they wade in, while fully clothed parents sit down in the shallow water, allowing the waves to wet them completely. The men have stripped down to their underwear. AC watches me staring at their groins. 'Excited?' he asks, sipping a beer. I nod. He walks towards a small group of stags—the ones staring lecherously at teenage girls in revealing swimwear. AC offers to buy them beer. They readily agree. I see him leading them towards my languorously reclining form. My bikini top is pulled down and my breasts are exposed. The men have hard-ons as they stare unabashedly at my upright nipples. AC is smirking—it's his knowing smile. When the men surround my deck chair, AC pours his half-finished beer over my breasts and says casually, 'I had promised you beer ... here it is ... go ahead ... drink it.' I throw my head back and surrender to the hungry mouths and tongues.

PART FIVE

DOUBLE WIDOW

It was a grand funeral. He had been a grand man. A man with a larger-than-life personality in all that he undertook. He was my lover for five short years. But during our time together, we had experienced many lifetimes. I was going to miss him. I heard her familiar, raspy voice, 'It's time you started behaving yourself as per your status and age ...'

That piece of worthless advice came from the grand man's wheelchair-bound spinster sister. 'I should have gone before my poor brother ...' she said between exaggerated sobs. 'After all, he was four years younger. He would have lived ... had he not met you.' I bent down, to meet her eyes, rested my hands on the arms of her wheelchair and said slowly, 'He was dead till he met me. He had been dead for years ... didn't you notice?'

~

Loneliness is a magnet. Loneliness attracts loneliness. I was lonely when we met. He had been lonely all his life. We merged our respective lonely selves, put them into a high-speed blender and made a smoothie out of them. We had known each other for decades. But not really known each other.

Each time we met, he would greet me with folded hands and say, 'Namastey, Deviji.' And each time I would tell him my name was not Devi. The conversation never varied.

He would smile (he had dimples) and say, 'It is out of respect ... I do know your name. Perhaps you also know mine—Jaivardhan. Friends call me Jai.'

'I am not your friend. And your name is too long. I will call you "Ji"—out of respect.' He would bow, do another elaborate namastey and move to another group. I never spotted a wife with him. I heard she did exist. I felt jealous of her even though he was nothing to me. A stranger in a city of strangers who pretend to be friends.

We kept running into one another at Marwari funerals. Lots of prominent Marwaris were dying that particular year, so our frequency of random namasteys went up. I had started looking out for him at prayer meetings. He was hard to miss with his towering height and piercing eyes. I think he too would search the mourners till he spotted me. He'd bow slightly, put his head down and leave with the men when the sabha ended. We did not speak. Till the day I ended up at the wrong funeral—rather, the wrong wing of the crematorium.

There were three bodies waiting to be cremated that morning. Two belonged to Marwaris. The third was Maharashtrian. One of the three electric furnaces had suddenly stopped functioning, leading to much confusion, with frantic family members running around the hall chasing harried office bearers. It was a strange situation. The cremations had been booked, scheduled and paid for well in advance. There was no point in demanding a refund—where would the uncremated bodies go?

The mourners got together and decided to settle the matter fairly by drawing lots. The Maharashtrian and one of the Marwaris got lucky. This upset the other Marwari family very much. They tried to do a deal with Marwari family #1.

Whose turn was next, by offering to pay for the entire expenses of their funeral if they let their body go first. 'It's a matter of forty-five minutes ... max one hour. These furnaces are fired and ready. The heat is already high. Besides, our family is expecting a lot of VVIPs. How can we keep such important people waiting because one of the furnaces is not working? Where will they sit? All the plastic chairs are taken. How will they park their cars in this small parking lot? We have arranged for a special bandobast for VVIP movement. Your mourners can use it while you wait.' A hasty consultation followed with the male members of the first Marwari family going into a huddle. Five minutes later, a young man wearing smart sunglasses and speaking with a heavy American accent approached the elders of Marwari family #2.

'I'm sorry guys ... But my folks want us to go ahead. I am here from the U.S. for my dad's funeral. I need to fly out tonight. Really sorry, but ...' Marwari Family #2 would have none of it. One of the men walked up to the young man, put an arm around his shoulder and took him to a side. Five minutes later, he came back with a smug smile, nodding his head and telling his priests to proceed with the last rites.

I entered just then and was about to join the other Marwari group when I spotted the Great Man. He bowed and indicated I should walk over to the other lot. I hastily adjusted my dupatta which had slipped off my shoulders, as I apologised to this group for intruding and rushed over to see 'our' body being placed on the fast track (as I called the tracks that led to the inferno and the gates of hell). I folded my hands to bid goodbye to someone whose name I didn't recall, and turned around to join the ladies briefly before leaving for the long trek back. These damn funerals were getting on my nerves. I wondered why I bothered to show up.

Just then, I caught the Great Man's eye and he smiled a slow, sweet smile ... I wanted to grab him and declare instant love. He looked so good in his off-white silk kurta, with floppy silk pyjamas. His bare feet were immaculate! Well-shaped, with evenly spaced toes, no hair sprouting here and there and well cared for toenails. I had always had a thing about feet and toes. Dead Squirrel's feet were like works of art—exquisite! These came a close second.

As I was getting into the car, I heard his voice asking, 'May I request the pleasure of your company over tea at the Willingdon Club? We could meet there in an hour.'

I replied, 'I love your feet.' He looked down, wiggled his toes and agreed whole heartedly, 'So do I! Does that mean a "Yes"?'

I said, 'Yes. But no tea. I'll have a gin and tonic.'

When I walked into the snobbiest club in India, I could feel several pairs of eyes scrutinising me. These were the 'regulars'—Parsee grande dames and Gujarati matrons, who were there every afternoon, playing bridge, or just sitting around on the verandah tinkling little bells to summon the 'Boy' (fifty year olds) and ordering mint tea and cucumber sandwiches. The Great Man stood up and went into his 'Namastey Deviji', routine, much to my annoyance.

'Let's stick to "Ji". You can call me Ji and I will call you Ji as well. Easy to remember. I am Ji and you are also Ji. That will make us equal-equal.' He smiled and asked if I still wanted that G and T. I did. We went towards the bar, and could feel all those eyes boring holes into our retreating backs.

'You come here often?' I asked just to make conversation. Suddenly, I had absolutely nothing to say to this man. I wanted to leave.

'Would you rather leave, Ji?' he asked giving me a start.

'Wait a minute Ji—what are you? A mind-reader?'

He shrugged, 'Yes. Since you asked ...' And that's how we became friends.

Our dates were ridiculously and disappointingly old-fashioned—concerts at Tata Theatre, dinners at the Taj, drives to Khandala (where he had a sprawling estate), art openings and the occasional party hosted by mutual friends (too polite, too dull). It was mind-numbingly tame and fake-civilised. After a few months of this routine, I asked myself whether I was with him because there was no one else on the scene. I was pretty alone and isolated those days. Or, was he more a girlfriend than a boyfriend? We had been going out on a regular basis for four months and still not had sex. That was odd. But in a way, it was also a huge relief. There was no sexual tension before an evening. So I didn't care about which bra and pair of panties to pick, or which fragrance to wear. It was chaste and safe and minus sparks. Maybe he couldn't get it up? I thought it best to ask and get the matter out of the way. We were driving to his friend's home at Juhu. He was at the wheel of his favourite vintage car (he had a museum-worthy collection).

At a traffic signal in Bandra, in front of the famous kebabwalla's stall, I turned to him and asked, 'Do you have any sex problem?'

He shook his head and replied, 'No ... not really. Why do you ask Ji?'

I paused, 'Because we haven't done it yet ... and I find that very odd.'

He smiled and reached for my hand, 'It's not odd at all ... do you want us to spend a night together? We can forget this dinner and drive to Khandala right now.'

'Let's!' I said with genuine enthusiasm. He called the staff there and told them to prepare two rooms. And organise dinner. 'No lobsters, I'm afraid! Just what the cook can put together in an hour. He and his wife have been with the family for twenty years. They are wonderful and will take good care of you.'

I reached out and touched his face. 'I really, really, really want someone to take good care of me—your cook and his wife will do. I am so tired of taking care of myself.' We drove in silence, listening to jazz and Bhimsen Joshi. There was no awkwardness, and I was mentally geared to accept whatever the night threw up.

~

'We observe certain formalities here. Some sort of a quaint, old-fashioned protocol,' the Great Man explained, as we drove through the heavy, wrought iron gates leading to the sprawling bungalow. I spotted a small lake on the property, surrounded by weeping willows.

'My wife's idea ...' he said, following my eyes. Wife! First time he had used that word. I quickly checked with Dead Squirrel whether I should still go ahead with this night plan or have dinner and flee? Dead Squirrel said to stay. So I stayed. Good decision. The cavernous living room with high ceilings was brimming over with old Kathiawari furniture. I loved the sankheda sofas and the gigantic Pichwais on the wall. The servants were well trained and discreet, and the cook also doubled up as a maali, he proudly told me, while his wife rolled out rotis and was in charge of the Bada Saab's breakfast.

'Bhabhiji didn't eat eggs.' Didn't. Not doesn't. I hoped she was dead. And had been dead for years. Why was I feeling possessive about a man I barely knew? I should have known about his wife—whether she was dead or alive. But stupidly, I didn't! Had I asked my mother-in-law, his entire family tree would have been produced in minutes. But then, her antenna would also have been alerted. She was a sharp thing, that chudail. She would have asked me, ghuma ke, of course, why these questions? And then kept tabs on me. I could have asked the Great Man directly. But actually, I didn't want to know. What if the wife existed? I would have felt silly dating one more married man. Out of sight, out of mind, was the best policy. It had always worked for me.

Besides, our conversations were invariably limited and pretty impersonal—maybe deliberately so. Perhaps we were both avoiding intimacy and involvement, or had forgotten what either meant. But my being with him tonight had already damaged that pantomime. 'Listen Ji ... I want to talk about your wife. I feel it's overdue. You already know I don't have a husband ... so there's nothing to hide. At the moment, I don't have a boyfriend, either …' Dead Squirrel was egging me on. I asked boldly, 'Can your maali get me some grass? I mean those funny cigarettes … weed?'

The Great Man said, 'Of course. Give me a minute.'

He came back ten minutes later with two joints in his hand, 'Down the road … the old paanwalla. Good stuff …' He lit one and handed it to me. I took a deep drag and so did he.

'Dead.' He said. 'To answer you.'

'What is dead? Who is dead?' I blurted, thinking he didn't approve of the freshness of the weed. He pointed to a silver-framed wedding picture on a sideboard.

'My wife. Rani Ishwar. She was from a small thikhana in Saurashtra. She died seven years ago. Good woman. Much loved by all.'

'Show!' I wanted to see a bigger, better picture. Close up. He held my hand and walked me into one of the bedrooms—his, I presumed. There, hanging over his large bed was her portrait—an oil, painted by a famous British portraitist. We were silent. The door had been softly shut behind us.

Ji held out his hand, 'I am here to take care of you, Ji,' he said solemnly, 'that's a promise.'

My head was spinning after five deep drags. 'So … that means I won't need your maali and his wife, right? To take care of me?'

Ji helped me out of my high heels, gently placed my feet on the bed and got in after me, 'Good Night, Ji,' he said and turned off the bedside light. I could hear the maali and his wife clearing up outside. We hadn't eaten their hastily cooked dinner. This was more important. I went to sleep dreaming of the lake ... I was floating across it in a decorated boat. Ji was on the other side.

We did not have sex that night. Or any other night after. As in proper sex-sex. It just did not happen. And it did not matter.

I discovered sleep. It was better than the best sex. That kind of sleep—deep, dreamless and mainly, minus sexual tension. I had grown tired of being with men I couldn't sleep soundly with. I had outgrown 'that' need—will we do it now? Or later? I'd discovered I could lie naked in bed with an attractive, robust man, and not miss sex. Sex, as in traditional sex. In and out, piston-type, penetrative sex. I was introduced to a varied and wonderful world of non-sex, sex. Of touch and smells and tastes and sound that went beyond 'screwing'.

We feasted on beauty. This was love making at its most tender—gentle, sensuous and satisfying. Ji and I moved into a pattern we both found joyful and complete. We read poetry in bed, watched movies and shows, listened to Bade Ghulam Ali, slept with our fingers entwined ... if Ji had a problem getting an erection, it was too delicate a subject to discuss ... and honestly speaking, did I have a choice? I never felt his erection, so I suppose, he didn't get one. But as a lover, he knew how to pleasure me like no man I had ever known. He was tireless and tuned in, making me feel so wobbly by the end of our passionate trysts, I forgot he had a penis. Or that I missed one.

The Great Man had been an adventurer. A big risk-taker. But in our relationship, he was neither. I found his composure restful. I was getting tired of seeking thrills myself. And his calmness soothed me. I still lusted after the odd fellow, of course. But checked myself instead of jumping into the sexual well as I had in the past. It was enough to stare at the butts of cops at the airport—those fit chaps in khaki, wearing perfectly tailored uniforms. Sometimes, on my international travels, I would deliberately include a few banned items, like lighters and scissors, just to linger a bit at security checks. Making eyes at men in uniform was an old habit. I was told it had to do with my longing for a figure of authority in my life. Someone else said, imposing men in general, attracted me because I missed Babuji while growing up.

Cock and bull, I tell you! Why is it so hard to accept a much easier explanation? I liked sex. And I liked men. Especially macho men. I imagined being in bed with them since I was a teenager, certain they would be good lovers. A bogus belief. So what? I used to point them out to Ji. And he would smile fondly and shake his head. He never asked if I had sex with other men. And I knew he didn't sleep with any other woman. The Khandala bungalow had become 'our' home. And I was treated like the mistress of the house by everybody—the maali, his wife, the two chauffeurs, local friends, the bearer who would come a day earlier to spruce up the place. Strange, but for the first time in my life, I felt I had a home of my own. I started to potter around the garden, and plant shrubs and trees of my choice. I got a beautiful old marble bird bath and fountain from a dealer in Chor Bazaar, and watched flocks of noisy parrots frolicking happily during summer, while I sat sipping nimbu paani on the verandah. Ji was not always with me, and it didn't matter. I felt content. That's what mattered.

I had let my business slide. Which was not such a smart thing. It was running the way Kushal decided it should. He was lazy, easily distracted and far from motivated. He was also doing drugs. As was Khushboo. I asked him once, when he didn't show up at the office for three straight days. And he blinked stupidly. So, I gave him one tight slap. Then a few more. Once I started slapping him, I couldn't stop. It was years of pent up frustration. I should have slapped him long ago. When at the age of five he had set fire to his toys he said he had done it 'just for fun'! Fun ka baap! I had restrained myself since Dead Squirrel said he would take care of it. Of course Dead Squirrel couldn't or didn't. His idea of punishing the children was to deny them pocket money for a week. They'd laugh openly and take it from their uncles and grandparents.

Anyway ... while I was slapping Kushal, his personal valet walked in and raised an alarm. 'Bhabhiji pagal ho gayi hai. She is killing Bhaiya ...' he screamed and ran out to get help. Kushal's nose was bleeding. His left cheek was puffed up and he looked like a mess. I felt nothing. No remorse seeing my son in that state. I wanted to beat him more. He was whimpering and crying. I yelled, 'Bloody chutiya ... stop your drama. Saala!'

At that very moment, my mother-in-law walked in with the cook, maids and security guard. She stared at me coldly and said, 'I can call the police right now and report the assault. But that will bring public disgrace to our family. It will make headlines. I can also have you sent to an asylum for your act of lunacy and violence. That will also bring disgrace on us. Don't think we didn't know about your mother and her madness. We knew everything. Still we took you into our home thinking, "Kuch nahi hoga." Now look!'

Kushal was lying on the carpet, doubled up and howling. He had wet his pants and his valet was looking for fresh clothes in his gigantic walk-in closet. Fortunately, his sister, the other druggie, was not at home. Or else, I would have beaten her to pulp as well. My mother-in-law was standing at a safe distance, as if expecting me to attack her. I didn't want to waste my blows on this rubber duck. I started laughing. At all of them. That confused her. She called the security guard and said, 'Hatao isko.'

I picked up a lamp from the bedside table and waved it at the small group saying, 'If you take one more step towards me, I will break this on your head.' She gestured to the others to step back. The security guard—burly and butter-fingered, dropped his danda out of nervousness. I thought he would also pee. He kept repeating, 'Bhabhiji ... Bhabhiji ... bas karo ... ruko.'

I raised the lamp in my hand and pretended I was going to hurl it at him. He fled. As did the others. But my mother-in-law was not done. She stood in the corridor, a good ten feet away and screamed, 'Get out! Just get out! Leave right now. Pack your things and get out. We have had enough of you. We all know my poor son was killed by you. Now you want to kill my grandson. You are worse than a rakhshas. Blood-sucking randi. You have muddied the good name of our family. Now—out! Enough of your immorality, you gutter woman from the streets of Kolkata. Neech aurat. Our entire community will disown you—not just this family. Then see what happens.'

I felt nothing.

There was nothing to feel. I had never belonged to this house in the first place. The children did not feel like my own. As for the community! Ha ... I would show them what a Marwari woman is capable of when she's left to her own devices. When she is left alone.

~

'Ji ... can you come and get me?' My voice was strong and calm.

'Of course, Ji. Where from?'

'This fucking mansion where I live. I'm leaving.'

The Great Man paused. 'Should I organise a van … or …?'

'For now, I just need you.'

'Be right there … give me half,' he replied. Equally strong and equally calm. I lay down on my bed for the last time. And spoke to Dead Squirrel. I asked him whether he also thought I had killed him. 'Never!' he assured me. That's all I wanted to hear. The next step was mine alone.

Ji was not in the car. I felt let down. The chauffeur was unfamiliar as well. Some new chap. English-speaking. 'Sir has told me to drive straight to Khandala. He has sent a packed lunch and soft drinks in this hamper.' I thanked him and got him to load two suitcases and a few pouches with my bags, handbags and shoes into the car. Next, I gave him directions to stop at the nearest liquor vendor. I got out of the car and ordered a case of wine, twenty-four cans of beer, two bottles of gin, one of vodka and one of whiskey. Then we stopped at a store I often used to buy smuggled imported foodstuff. He had only two tins left of Beluga and five of some unknown Caspian Sea caviar. I bought the lot. I needed the best bread and found it with a local baker. 'Let's go …' I said to the new chauffeur.

The party had just begun.

I was drunk out of my skull when the car rolled into the Khandala bungalow. I have no recall of what I drank or how much. I know I had offered to share everything, glass for glass, with the chauffeur, and insisted on him saying 'Cheers!' with each refill. The car stereo was blasting

'Carmen'—an opera I loved to listen to with Ji—when I staggered out of the open door, pretending to be the matador who jilts Carmen. I was waving an imaginary red cape, imagining an enraged wounded bull charging when I lost my balance and fell face down on the pebbles in the porch. Maria Callas was singing the final aria … and here I was lying piss drunk, sprawled out at the entrance of my future home.

'Namastey maaliji …' I slurred. I assured the maali and his wife that I was just fine … I also added I hadn't killed anybody. Just in case they thought I was running away from some terrible crime. The maali's wife escorted me to the bedroom and gave me a bucket bath—the best kind of bath in the world. Yes, she saw me naked. I didn't care. I was still singing. Dinner had been ordered, but I refused to eat. I wanted to share their dinner with them in the kitchen. I pleaded and pleaded … and while I was still pleading away, I heard a car driving in. Ji was here. Or so I thought. It was the local police.

I heard the maali and the chauffeur arguing with the cops. I also overheard a few phone calls. The words 'unruly conduct' and some section under which I was to be arrested were being discussed. Ridiculous! I went outside and tried to grab the phone out of the senior cop's hands. 'Let me speak … I want to talk to the prime minister. Right now! Get him on the line … listen to me. Pradhan mantri ji ke saath baat karni hai …'

The smart chauffeur was taking instructions from Ji—I

assumed. But no! He was talking to Ji's lawyer. Twenty minutes later, the cops left. I ate up the maali's dinner of bajra bhakri, roasted onions, lasoon dry chutney, methi, plus a matka of dahi. I offered them caviar. They politely refused. My new life had just begun.

~

Ji arrived two days later. I was glad for the time to myself. I slept a lot. Listened to music. Planted new rose bushes. Watched the birds. And plotted. Dead Squirrel had disappeared. Gone silent. Maybe he was finally done with me. Or maybe he had found Soumitro. I was feeling cancelled. Rejected. But not upset. How long could Dead Squirrel keep looking out for me? Even he needed a break. It was time I learned to live alone. But for that, I needed funds. With my business out of my hands after the Kushal episode, there was no choice left but to sell the Delhi bungalow. There go my two olives, I laughed. My martini days were long over. Sell ... or leverage? I decided to borrow money and use the property as collateral. I had to do this quickly and on my own. Ji offered to help me out financially and pitch in with a generous inflow of funds, till I got my bearings. But I refused.

This was my battle. And I wanted to fight it my way—minus obligations. Ji understood. Or didn't. I never asked. But thanks to him, I had a roof over my head and was well taken care of by the kindness of his staff. I didn't have to worry about khaana peena ... and that was a huge bonus. Ji would visit when able, and that worked, too. In his own way he was living up to his original promise of looking after me. Ma's Mental Wellness Foundation was in excellent hands. I had kicked out Khushboo—she desperately needed to check into a clinic before she could assume any responsibility. My small team was doing a good job and raising funds on their own through art and fashion events. They had successfully persuaded a top star to become the brand ambassador, and I was required to oversee the project, which was not difficult or taxing to do.

About three months into this new life in Khandala, my business plans were still up in the air. I had met a few property developers from Bombay, who were keen to explore Khandala, Lonavala, Mulshi, Pawana, Pune and nearby areas which were still lush and verdant and untouched. The potential was vast. The market was also on an upswing with positive global cues. A few famous film stars had bought ten acres and more near Ji's property and started an exclusive gated community with Malibu-style villas, complete with Jacuzzis and multiple pools, a club house and health club. I got to know two of them and discovered I had a nose for property. I could drive around by myself for hours in the hills and spot a site worth investing in. I was also good with visualizing what a canny developer could do with a well-located, underpriced property.

Through the maali, I had access to the required

information about which farmer owned what land. The maali's ancestors had lived in these villages for generations and tilled tiny patches of land. He had a large network of relatives with small land holdings—they were willing to sell to a trusted party. I was that party. I started small, buying one or two acres a go. In under a year, I owned over one hundred acres. With the maali's connections at the tehsildar's office, I managed to complete the tedious paperwork in record time.

Of course, I always compensated the maali—we were now growing more than just rose bushes together! And thanks to his wife, I picked up sufficient Marathi to talk to the farmers and the government clerks in charge of pushing files, and registered all the land deeds swiftly. Soon, city buyers looking for luxury weekend homes started approaching me directly. The money started coming in at a good lick. Lots of it. And my health, which had taken a hit after that Kushal nonsense, started to pick up. I had temporarily stopped drinking—not that booze was ever a big thing for me. But I realised quickly if I wanted to go for the kill, my head had to be bilkul clear. And all my faculties, razor sharp. My deals were clean, above board and quick.

Unlike rival brokers who indulged in all kinds of underhand practices, I had decided to keep my business as sanitized as I could—given its dirty nature. Soon, I acquired a small team—one Marwari, one Punjabi and one Maharashtrian. It was a magic combo! Ruthless meets gutsy meets down to earth. I called my company 'Carmen Infrastructure'. I was the wild, adventurous gypsy. But, afsos ki baat that there wasn't a single sexy matador in sight! 'Carmen' had saved me that fateful night. It was her spirit that had kept me going ... along with all the other spirits I had recklessly consumed!

I still missed hard, old-fashioned sex. But with menopause approaching, my libido was slowing down, mercifully, just a teeny weeny bit, much to my distress. This menopause business was a bloody nuisance, I tell you. All those mood swings and sluggish feelings. But men still hit on me, and I flirted right back! I had nothing to lose. Nobody was going to impregnate me. And I was not looking for love or marriage or stability or money or anything. For the first time in my life, I was truly free—and carefree! I had sold some of my heirloom jewellery and invested in land with the money. I had also started selling a few canvases from the extensive art collection Squirrel and I had acquired.

Luckily, we had bought the masters at sensible prices, at the right time. Some of the works had appreciated in such a crazy way, I couldn't believe the numbers reputed auction houses were offloading them at to art bakras—those idiots who wanted to buy a canvas for the famous signature on it, and nothing else. Or those junglees, those unpadhs, the art illiterates who bought art by the square inch. Good for me! I didn't want to leave anything for either Khusboo or Kushal. They didn't deserve a penny, forget my precious art or jewellery. The money I now possessed was substantial. And it was all for me! Land was getting sexier and sexier as an investment option. My stocks were rock solid.

Looked at from any angle, I had made it! I could afford to gloat. And did so shamelessly. Away from the incestuous social scene of Bombay, I felt completely unshackled and happily reinvented my identity. I became a Khandalawali. My surname didn't matter, I did. Nobody asked me silly, unnecessary questions about my husband or the absence of one. I was accepted as the wild woman who tore around the hills in a Jeep, and fed stray dogs Glucon-D biscuits. My hair was short and mannish. People thought I was a lesbian. I wore dungarees and boots, and had taken rifle shooting lessons at the range. I acquired an arms' license soon after, and locals knew I was a bandookwali who wouldn't hesitate to shoot. Of course, there were all kinds of rumours about me. Some said I had murdered my mother-in-law (I wish!), others said I had poisoned my husband (sweet Dead Squirrel ... never!), and of course everyone knew I had bloodied my druggie son and disowned my druggie daughter. Good, they knew! Being badnaam had its advantages.

The maali's wife had become my confidante of sorts (she had seen me stark naked—there was nothing left to hide), so one day I asked her, 'Do the villagers think I am mad? Crazy? Pagal?' She thought for a bit and said, 'Yes. But not in a bad way. They think you should stand for Zilla Parishad elections … you have done so much for these people. Got them water, made toilets, started a school for girls … we will all vote for you, madamji.'

I laughed, 'Which party will support me?' She answered seriously, 'My father-in-law's.'

Ji was amused. 'Do it,' he said laconically. We were lolling in bed watching Steve McQueen. We watched all his movies over and over again, but *The Thomas Crown Affair* was Ji's favourite. He was sipping a Merlot and seemed unusually mellow.

'How's the new villa project coming along?' he asked, caressing the back of my neck.

'Happening,' I answered without going into the details. It was understood we wouldn't get into each other's business decisions. He nodded. My adopted stray Spartacus, walked in for a quick belly rub and a treat. When Ji was not around, Spartacus slept in the room with me, snoring contentedly in his doggy bed, while I snored in mine. Spartacus must have sensed something was off, because he started whining. I thought he had spotted an unfamiliar object under the bed, or maybe a garden rat had sneaked in—though that had never happened in all these years.

'Sparky! Stop it … come here … what's the matter?' He tried to scramble up on the bed—from Ji's side. He had never done that! Strange. The whining increased—it was prolonged and high-pitched. Ji reached over to pat Spartacus … and the very next moment I heard a huge thud. Ji had keeled over and was lying motionless on the carpet. I screamed and ran to summon help. The maali's wife rushed over, placed her index finger under Ji's nostrils, looked up at me and said, 'Alive! He is alive ... madam, please call the ambulance. I will call my father-in-law.'

Ji was moved to the local hospital in minutes. He'd suffered a stroke, but his other parameters were reasonably strong, the doctors assured me. What did that even mean? All I could see was a lifeless—and they were saying he would be okay? 'At the moment, he is stable, madam. That's all we can say. We are monitoring him.'

I wanted to shift him to a better, larger, more modern hospital in Bombay, but the doctors said he couldn't be moved. It seemed so bizarre, this Great Man and us—a maali, his wife and me—watching him anxiously, while his chest moved rhythmically up and down, and everything else was frozen.

'Will he die?' I asked the maali, like he was the most acknowledged neurologist on earth. He looked at Ji's face and then back at me. 'Not so soon, madam. Not so soon,' he said.

'How do you know?' I asked. The maali answered, 'I have seen many deaths. I recognise death ... death has yet to arrive.'

'Does that mean he may die later tonight? Tomorrow? When?' Once again, the maali stared at Ji steadily and said, 'Not tonight. Not tomorrow. It will take time.

Maybe months. Maybe years. Death is not ready just now. Undecided. Kuch nakki nahi hai, madamji.'

~

Death was not ready to take Ji. But his family was ready to finish me. On being informed by the maali of the cerebral haemorrhage suffered by the Great Man, his wheelchair-bound sister, ironically named Sneh Rani (queen of love), asked just one question: 'Where is the witch?'

I prompted the maali to say I was right there, by his side and not moving an inch. She slammed down the phone and we went back to our vigil. There was zero improvement. But the doctors kept saying, 'He's stable. He's stable.' I was stable, too. Very stable. Shaken, yes. But stable. Moving him to Breach Candy, under the able care of the senior-most specialist, was my priority number one. I had made the calls and sought an appointment on a priority basis. But before any of this could happen, Wheelchair arrived with an entourage of cackling women—staff or relatives, was hard to say.

Maali and wife bowed low and all but prostrated themselves at her feet. I was in shorts. Sneh Rani glared, then stared at my bare legs. I felt like pulling my shorts down and showing her what she really wanted to see! It must have been ages since she saw female or male sexual parts. She looked around the place as if to check if I had stolen any of the precious 'objets' strewn around. She summoned the maali and asked in an imperious tone where the Great Man's wallet and watch were.

He nodded in my direction and mumbled, 'Unke paas.'

She snapped, 'Please return our belongings immediately ... or else I shall call the police. The police commissioner is our family friend.'

I said, 'Call him!'

She cursed under her breath and told the maali to unpack her saaman. 'We will be living here henceforth, please organise the kitchen accordingly. Inform the dhobi, get the old jamadaars back. I hear they were dismissed.' Maali looked uncertainly at me. 'Why are you looking at that woman? This is not her house—it is our home. Pack her belongings and throw her out. Right now.'

I had not moved from the entrance of 'our' bedroom—mine and Ji's. Sparky was next to me, emitting low growls and had earlier attempted to sniff the wheelchair. I had hoped he'd pee on it and her, but unfortunately, he was a bit too well bred to do that. The maali's wife came in carrying a tray of lemonade, along with a plate of locally baked biscuits which Ji loved with his morning tea.

Sneha Rani looked disdainfully at them and snorted, 'Since when did my brother acquire such ganwar taste? Our biscuits come from London. He has never eaten anything but the shortbreads from Harrod's.' I was silently watching. Waiting. The cackling entourage was walking from room to room, oohing and aahing over marble statues and crystal vases. One or two were strolling around in the garden, smelling my roses. *My roses!* They had already made themselves at home. I summoned the maali and his wife and spoke to them audibly.

I wanted to be heard. 'Please connect me to your father-in-law,' I told the maali's wife. She got 'Bhau' on the line and handed me the phone.

I said slowly, 'Bhau Saheb ... I need a few of your men here at my home, please. Yes, it's urgent. There are intruders from Bombay who are creating a disturbance and refusing to leave. Yes, they are trespassers. About ten men should be sufficient. Yes ... as soon as possible. I am waiting.'

Painless, quick and efficiently done. Pest control. But at a bhaari price. The vermin would be back. Cockroaches are indestructible.

~

Ji's recovery was slow, but with each new blink and movement, I felt like we were both winning bout after boxing bout. I felt Ji knew I was right there, next to his propped up pillows, talking constantly, occasionally humming, but constantly connecting. Ji was not allowed visitors just yet. But dozens of former colleagues and employees called every day to check on him. Sneh Rani did not call or visit. His old, trusted secretary became my contact with the world outside the hospital. He was there to handle bank work, withdraw cash, monitor what was what, help me fill those awful forms and deal with nurses, particularly on days when my energy levels were low and I needed a break for a few hours.

During one of my mini breaks, while I was enjoying a chicken roll and wondering whether to get my legs waxed, I met an interesting person. Of course, it had to be a man—come on! Menopause or no menopause, I was still a straight woman! Everything was in working order—I mean everything. I had eyes—so I noticed men! They also noticed me noticing them. It was always a lovely moment of mutual recognition. There was nothing cheap about any of it. Swear! What was there to feel guilty about? I wasn't doing anything—just looking. Not even touching. I was missing Ji's cuddles and touches, and honestly speaking, I wasn't really cut out to be the loving-caring-selfless Florence Nightingale type. I was pretty bored, pretty restless. Even though I wasn't actively looking-looking to flirt with strangers, if a man accidentally found me at a chicken roll stall, and he was also eating a chicken roll, obviously, we'd start a conversation.

Just that: a conversation. About different chicken rolls in the city, and where one could find the best one—with mayonnaise, without mayonnaise, with mustard and mayonnaise, grilled and diced chicken filling, or just marinated slices. There's so much to discuss when it comes to chicken rolls. So, after that first short conversation, I started taking daily chicken roll breaks from my hospital duty. I suppose he also couldn't stay away from chicken rolls.

We became chicken roll friends. He was a kid. Not a kid-kid. But compared to my age, every young man was a kid. I liked his cheeky humour and that he didn't call me 'Aunty'. Not once. He was a boy-man. Naughty and immature, playful and childish. His language was so new, filled with slang I had never heard ... I was tempted to adopt him. I didn't have any contact with my awful son, in any case. Why not this chap? For that, I needed to win him over and get his confidence. Without Dead Squirrel to guide me, I was left to stumble through all the messes in my life on my own. Some were created by me, others, I was stuck with. Ji's hospital bills were mounting steadily. Not that I minded footing them. But the entire extended hospital stay was pulling me down, financially and emotionally.

'Chicken Roll' was a welcome distraction.

~

'I am a half-Bawaji,' Chicken Roll told me, on a gloomy monsoon day. 'Which half?' I asked, trying not to sound cheap. He laughed, picked up his loose tee and displayed his taut six-pack—'This half!' Before I could stop myself, I had allowed my eyes to pop out of their sockets, and my tongue to hang out. Disgusting!

I mouthed, 'Wow!' (Shameless slut!) And bit into my chicken roll greedily. He leaned over and carefully removed a blob of gooey mayonnaise from the corner of my mouth with his index finger. Next, he licked the mayonnaise off his finger with a wicked grin, 'Why waste good mayonnaise? That's what my mother always says, "Never waste good stuff."' Mother! Maybe she was my age? Possibly younger.

'Parsee? Your mother?' He nodded. 'Yes! And gorgeous. Used to fly for Air India, then British Airways. Met my pilot dad—and khattam. One of those love stories. My dad is a Panju. Solid Panju. Cut Surd. Full on Balle Balle types. They fight all the time. But I am not bothered. I get my amazing looks from both of them—my dad's physique, and my mom's beauty.' I overlooked the immature bragging and tried to control my jealousy. Chicken Roll was so sure, so confident, so sure of himself, so happy and carefree! He hadn't mentioned a girl-friend so far. I was dying to ask. But this wasn't the time—he was on his mom-dad-and-me track.

And I had to rush back to the hospital. The physiotherapist was coming soon, and Ji would ask for me, now that his speech was coming back gradually. I could understand what he was saying, and one or two of the nurses had also figured out his words, but nobody else could. And that made my job very taxing. I loved Ji and all that. But I was not sure how long I'd be able to maintain this vigil before cracking myself. Just to relieve the monotony of our conversation, which didn't go beyond which tablet to take, and what exercise worked best, I decided to tell him about Chicken Roll.

'I met a really sweet boy at the snack place down the road,' I said conversationally. He wiggled his eyebrows and gave me a lop-sided grin. He tried to join his thumb and index finger to make an 'okay' sign, gave up and tried a thumbs up. I leaned over and kissed his drooly mouth and gave him a big hug. 'He's a kid—a bachcha,' I added unnecessarily.

Ji smiled some more. Oh God! I had just described Chicken Roll as a 'bachcha'. And I lusted after him! Had I become a Dirty Old Woman? Ugh! I wanted to show Ji a photograph of Chicken Roll. But wasn't sure how to click it without looking stupid.

The next day, I reached late. Chicken Roll had come and left. The man at the counter said, 'Baba gayaa. Madam ke liye bahut wait kiya, aur phir gaya. Yeh diya hai, aapke liye.' I wanted to burst into tears. Baba. Madam. I was a Dirty Old Woman. Even the scruffy fellow at the counter knew it. I felt let down and disappointed. What if I never saw Chicken Roll again? All I knew was rubbish stuff. I didn't even know his name! Or address.

I took the crumpled paper napkin from the snack counter man's grubby hands. There! Gotcha! It had a number on it. And a short message. It said: 'Lady, call me.' It was signed, 'Bawaji'. Idiot. He could have given his real name. I kissed the paper napkin passionately.

Then I performed a little dance—right there on the pavement. A few people stared. But people always stared at me. These days I wore denim shorts with sleeveless ganjis. I called it my 'hospital' uniform. But I know I looked bloody good when I walked down that corridor. Even the nurses used to compliment me and say, 'Madam, you look too cute.' Chicken Roll must have thought I was cute, too.

I dialed and he answered immediately. 'Hi! This is the Lady on the line,' I announced. I heard him chuckle.

'Navroz Mubarak', he added. It was the Parsee New Year. 'Let's watch a movie,' he suggested, 'And after that, we can go to the club for a swim.'

Was he serious? Did he think he was setting up a college date? I jumped at it! Woweeeee. Hadn't done anything like this ever! I mean, not even when I was in college myself. We agreed to meet at Metro Cinema. Having agreed, I was stuck. And there was a problem. I was to meet Ji's doctors for a consultation. The doc was a superstar. It had taken me ten days and some serious string pulling to get an appointment. Forget it! I said and called the doctor's secretary to cancel. I felt no guilt. No regret. I rushed to the hospital, ran up the stairs, went to the nurses' station and fibbed I had a family issue to deal with. I rushed into Ji's room, flung myself on his prone, still body and announced cheerfully, 'Ji ... I am going on a date with that bachcha I told you about. Okay? I'll see you tomorrow. Be a good boy and take your medicines without fussing. Don't give the nurses a hard time! Eat your custard. Sleep well. Byeeeeeee.'

Fifteen minutes later I was at the Metro Cinema.

~

So began this light-hearted flirtation with Chicken Roll. A harmless fling I said to myself, each time we fixed a date and I lied to Ji. Nobody else knew or cared. And I was answerable only to myself. Who and what had I turned into? I regressed by the day. My appearance altered dramatically—even the nurses noticed and giggled.

One of them asked tartly, 'Madam looking cute only ... but these days wearing daughter's clothes, it seems.' I wanted to box her. Bitch!

I turned to her haughtily and said, 'This is the latest fashion, Sister.' I wanted to add, 'But how would you know, you cow from nowhere.' She had hit a raw nerve, and I knew I was kidding myself each time I hastily applied lip gloss going down the painfully slow hospital elevator, often accompanied by patients on stretchers, and other sick people. I noticed nothing and no one. Felt nothing even when someone in pain was groaning two feet away from me. I would breeze in an out of Ji's room, escaping as fast as I was able to.

Chicken Roll asked very few questions, and was a slam bam kind of lover. He liked my experienced ways, and I liked his raw energy. The setting was invariably shabby—

the backseat of his father's car, or a friend's empty home. It didn't matter. My emptiness appeared less empty when I was with him. And I felt rejuvenated listening to his music and talking about his favourite television shows. Chicken Roll took my mind off *me*! Or what was left of me. It was a whirlwind 'romance'—though, the romance was solely in my head. For the young boy, I was another lay—and such a stress-free one!

I made no demands, and neither did he. Driving around in his father's second-hand Merc, stopping to sample the latest flavour of frozen yogurt, or eat a messy, spicy vada pav with a chilled beer to go with it, took me back to a time I had never experienced as a college girl, but only read about, or seen in the movies. We held hands like teenage lovers, and stole kisses at the movies. When people stared in disbelief, Chicken Roll showed them his middle finger and I silently mouthed, 'Up yours!'

Defiance was always up there in my life ... being with this bratty kid was a part of some idiotic plan to 'show everybody'. Show what? My own damaged self? My self-inflicted wounds? I overheard a woman sniggering, 'Look at this old hag! Cradle-snatcher. Not even embarrassed ... he must be younger than her own son.' Maybe he was younger than Kushal—but as if a decade here or there makes such relationships either okay or not okay. For the two of us, it was perfectly okay.

Three months later, just like that, Chicken Roll ended it—whatever this 'it' had been. He called and said he was leaving for London. He had found a job as a purser, thanks to his father's old connections. There was no time to say goodbye. I wanted to give him a small gift and thank him for saving me at a time I was sinking into a slow but certain depression. I stopped eating chicken rolls after that … and haven't touched one since. Mayonnaise? No way!

~

Ji was discharged a few weeks later. I could never have taken care of him in Khandala. I gladly handed him over to his demon sister and their relatives. I, of course, paid the entire bill—they didn't as much as offer. I watched their cars driving up to the hospital gates. Now there would be two wheelchairs in that grander-than-grand family mansion. Not my problem. I had said my goodbye to Ji that morning. And taken his watch as a keepsake. I started to wear it on my wrist, to remind me of this very kind and loving man I had had the good fortune to spend a few years with. He had demonstrated the beauty and power of dignity in countless little acts that would stay with me forever. Ji had made me feel valued for something far more than my body. I had kept a photograph of the two of us in Khandala, near the rose bushes, next to the bird bath. I needed to go back to say a final goodbye to Sparky, the maali and his wife. And to tell them I was sorry I couldn't stand for the Zilla Parishad elections, but

I deeply appreciated their trust and faith in my abilities to contribute to the community. I also wanted to give them sufficient cash to build a home for themselves—that would free them from the tyranny of Sneh Rani and the rest, who constantly threatened to throw them out from the tiny, shabby cottage on the property.

I was glad I made that last trip. I stayed for a week. And was lovingly fed by both of them. Ji had slipped away quietly and with characteristic dignity at his family mansion after the doctors had informed the family there was nothing more they could do for him. When I read some of the obituaries which detailed Ji's many achievements, I smiled to myself. He was too well bred and modest to ever boast about his life or refer to his impressive track record as a dynamic business leader who had headed many corporate bodies, had been on several boards, and been honoured with a Padma Bhushan. He had been a pillar of the Marwari community, and highly respected for his ethical business practices.

I knew he had turned down a Rajya Sabha seat, unwilling to be indebted to the ruling power of the time. This had made him a big hero across India, especially when he had boldly criticized the Budget and questioned the government about its taxation policies. No wonder the prime minister had sent a wreath to be placed near his body at the crematorium. And two cabinet ministers had flown in from Delhi to pay their respects. I wondered whether any of this had ever really mattered to Ji. So many pompous people lived their lives dreaming about their own fancy funerals! Ji would have chuckled at the eulogies and hugged me saying, 'Who's this man? Sounds like an ass. Do you know him?'

I went back to the hospital to thank the nursing staff and those very kind ward boys who bathed Ji, changed him, brushed his teeth, given him a shave, made sure he didn't suffer from bed sores, and gave him the bedpan without once complaining. These were the people who had gone well beyond the call of duty and taken excellent care of my Ji. They were pleased to see me, I guess. I had carried a large chocolate cake with 'Thank You' written across it. And wafers, which I knew they loved. It was a sweet and apt farewell, complete in itself. Ji would have approved. Behind his public image, was a shy, simple man—the one I had fallen in love with. I wasn't surprised he had left the Khandala property to me in his will. But now that it was 'officially' mine, I didn't want it—I had no use for it. It had meaning as long as Ji had been alive. I discussed the issue with the maali and his wife. They felt the same way I did. Without Ji, they too were not interested in working for anybody else. It was decided we would put it up for sale. I was in no hurry.

My life was going to change yet again, and I had no idea what that change was likely to be. Lying on what was 'our' bed for the last and final time, a thought struck me. I had lost two wonderful men within a span of ten years—Squirrel and Ji. One, I had been married to, the other I was even more married to without even being married. Technically, I was a widow. Dead Squirrel's widow. But in my heart and mind, I was a double-widow. Maybe, I was born under the rare 'double-widow' star. The realisation did not make me feel bad. I still had some unfinished business to attend to. I checked Ji's watch, which was now on my wrist. I had just enough time to drive back to Bombay, and catch a flight up North. I knew where I wanted to say 'farewell' to Ji. Rishikesh was calling me ...

EPILOGUE

DEVIJI

Rishikesh

Sitting on the banks of the mighty Ganga, my feet trailing in the rapidly flowing water, I waited for the perfect moment. It would come a few minutes later, when the sun dipped behind the mountains, and hundreds of devotees lit diyas for the maha Ganga Aarti. I was going to light a diya, too. And fill it with a fistful of ashes. Ji's ashes. I had bribed one of the crematorium attendants to steal some for me. I smiled. I had had to pay a thousand rupees for collecting what remained of my lover—a small copper container of ash—and even that had come with a price tag. Would anybody bother to ask for my ash when the time came?

I had two more diyas with me—one was for Dead Squirrel. I had not really said an appropriate adieu to my 'other' or rather, only husband. This was my only chance as a 'double-widow' to follow my heart and say goodbye to the two men who had loved me the way I wanted to be loved. I wasn't blessed enough by my stars to die a 'sowbhagyawati'—every Hindu married woman's ultimate wish. Imagine! They all want to die before their husbands, with blood red sindoor in the parting of their hair, a mangalsutra round their necks, bangles on their wrists and flowers circling their nape bun—all the auspicious symbols of wedded bliss which are denied to widows when their pyres are lit.

The third diya was for me. I was certain nobody would light a diya in my memory when I was gone. So, better I lit it in advance for myself! I held the tiny diya for Ji in the palms of both my hands. It was so fragile! Anybody could crush my humble diya made out of two leaves firmly held together by twigs. This is what the devout float down the river every evening to honour its power and majesty, and to honour the dead. I would float mine too, and follow its journey till I lost sight of it, as it bobbed up and down with hundreds of other diyas. Each one, carrying a wish, a desire, a prayer. When all three diyas were in the water, I gave each one a slight push and saw mine overtake the other two—in life, so in death. I was ahead!

I was more alone than I had ever been in my life. Alone. Not lonely. Ji had taught me to value solitude, and during those long, silent hours by his hospital bed, I had had the luxury of undisturbed introspection. Today ... as I heard the chanting of the priests from the Parmath Ghat, and watched the flames from the huge, gleaming brass lamps flickering and dancing in the evening breeze, held aloft by tall, strapping, handsome Brahmins, I felt a strange stillness. This was new!

A stillness so soft and comforting, I thought my 'other' self was sitting next to me, saying, 'This is your time … all yours … grab it!' I sat for an hour or so at the far end of the ghat—away from the pilgrims and other mourners. It was a moonless night, and the chill was setting in as I walked back to the modest guest house I had booked for ten days. I passed some of the people who had attended the evening aarti and felt one with them. As if, some mysterious force was binding me to every human being on earth, all at once. The same force that had brought me here and was now urging me to stay for a while … linger … feel … surrender.

~

So … here I am ten years later … on the same ghat. But I am not the same woman. A lot has happened to me during this tumultuous decade. I fell seriously ill and was given up for dead, as I lay unmoving on the familiar mud-track that took me to the bazaar. A passing pilgrim picked me up and left me inside a nearby ashram. Why did I collapse? Was it pneumonia? Low blood sugar? Something even deadlier? I shall never know, nor is there any point in finding out. I survived! And that's what matters.

I was nourished back to good health by the sadhus

and sadhvis in the ashram. They were kind and patient as they watched me recuperate, never once questioning my presence. I made friends with a couple of sadhvis. One of them was Swiss and a Sanskrit scholar. They introduced me to a way of life that should have felt alien, but didn't. I started appreciating it over time. I need the discipline it provided—the regular hours and meditation, the daily seva and prayers, the sonorous chanting and the reading of world scriptures. Not once did anybody try and impose any kind of thinking on me. Nor was I questioned about my past. I was accepted! As easily and simply as I am stating it now. Minus any judgments. Since nobody knew my name, nor had anybody asked, I became 'Deviji'—in recognition of the devi in every woman. I accepted my new name enthusiastically—it was what Ji had called me when we first met. Maybe Ji had led me to this ashram. Maybe Ji was the guiding force. Maybe he had foreseen this life for me. Beloved Ji. My 'double-widow' Ji. But I knew I had found my final home.

I had stopped running.

~

So, what happened to the woman who had placed sex above all else in her life? The one for whom sex was more important than ... than ... well ... everything! Children, parents, husband, food, business, safety, reputation, religion, health ... sab kuch. I was not a sex maniac. Nor was I a nympho. I was just a woman with an appetite. A curious and adventurous woman. Unapologetic about expressing my desires. I loved cheese omelets. I loved sex. Simple. Sex gave me enormous pleasure—I was my best self while having sex.

Sex completed me. It enhanced my creativity like nothing else could. I made my best plans while making love—my brain was at its sharpest, and every instinct came alive while I gave myself up to the pure, uncomplicated, unadulterated sensations I was experiencing—every, tingling micro-second mattered. As I hoped it also mattered to my partner. I was not a selfish lover. I offered myself unconditionally—body, mind and soul. It was 'oneness' I sought. I was 100 per cent me during sex. But now, I was my own best lover—I didn't need another to feel appreciated. I had finally fallen in love with me.

And nothing changed at the ashram. None of this. I remained an avid seeker of sex. Except that I became far, far more aware of my own sexuality and my approach to sex itself altered. I no longer chased sex. Sex chased me. This freed me from old anxieties and let me soar into new dimensions, fly to new sexual worlds. I started to write and paint and sculpt. I became a potter for a while. Then a gardener. I designed jewellery. Held an exhibition of my photographs. Hiked. Tried white water rafting. The ashram was such.

I felt encouraged and confident to try my hand at

everything and anything, or even do nothing at all. Just be. One of my business ventures was a pure vegetarian pizzeria, which earned several glowing mentions on tourist websites. It's still running! I was proud of my strong Marwari genes. Never had I felt so damned grateful to have been born a Marwari—tough, hardy, resilient, practical and never afraid of taking a risk. The biggest, bloodiest risk! I was a Marwari chameleon—I could adapt, change, blend in. This is every Marwari's secret weapon. We can assimilate just like ghee assimilates with jaggery. Milk with sugar.

~

I woke up late this morning and took a good hard look at myself in the full length bathroom mirror. Hmmmm—what was there not to love? My breasts were bouncy, my butt taut (all that walking, hiking and cycling in the hills had paid off); my skin glowed thanks to the satvic diet. Alas, there was nobody to seduce over a G and T at the ashram—otherwise I would have sneaked in the forbidden bottle of alcohol, somehow. By now my hair was touched with interestingly scattered silver streaks, which I was told, gave me a great personality! But hey—I was never one for possessing a 'personality'. Let others opt for that, I would say. Give me uncut, unfiltered sexiness any day. Sexy I was, and sexy I remain. When I walk down to the bazaar in my thin, fiery saffron or pristine white robes, men stare, mouths agape, and then hastily look away. They feel guilty ogling a woman they think has taken sanyaas. Renounced wordly pleasures. Haaaah! Over my dead body!

If only they knew.

Acknowledgements

I didn't choose Srilaaji, Srilaaji chose me!

This is how it happened: My brand new publishers (Simon and Schuster India) had shown extraordinary faith in a book proposal that had been pitched to them by Asia's super successful literary agent, Kanishka Gupta. But, guess what? This is not that book! Srilaaji smoothly hijacked the project by overruling the original idea and replacing it with herself. Strange? Well, writers and their characters are strange creatures, so ...

Interestingly, that 'dumped' book was a non-fiction title we were all excited about. Himanjali Sankar (Editorial Director) and Sayantan Ghosh (Senior Commissioning Editor) had planned a quick trip to meet me in Mumbai, armed with the contract and ready to get the show on the road. We were to accomplish all this most efficiently and briskly over evening chai and sandesh at my home. But wait! Something dramatic happened in between.

It was close to 1 p.m. when right out of the blue Srilaaji 'appeared' before me and demanded to be the heroine of my next book. It was an order, not a request.

Imperious and impatient, seductive and disarming—this woman refused to leave! I swear I am not making any of this up. I surrendered to Srilaaji and did what I thought was the right thing: phoned Kanishka and broke it to him that the deal was off! I had changed my mind about writing the book and would he please let the publishers know? Kanishka exclaimed, 'Haiiiin?' and asked what had happened for me to do an about-turn at this late stage. I told him the truth. 'Srilaaji is with me right now … and I want to write her story.' Kanishka didn't laugh. Maybe he wept. But he was considerate enough to do so silently.

Next: A call from Himanjali. She was in Mumbai. Gulp. I told her the same thing. I mentioned Srilaaji's 'hukum'. I said I was really, really sorry but I didn't want to write non-fiction, after all. I insisted we keep our chai date regardless and meet at my home as planned, for that cuppa. Anybody who has ever interacted with Himanjali will tell you, the dimpled lady is an exceedingly polite ('bhadra' to the core) and well-brought-up person. So is the ever-upbeat, laid back Sayantan. Both of them arrived, grinning broadly and not making me feel weird at all. Over tea, I told them all about Srilaaji, and why I absolutely had to write this book and not that book. They looked at each other, smiled some more and said, 'Fine!' Heaven knows what they said to Rahul Srivastava, the big daddy at Simon and Schuster India, but hey! We were back in business!

Srilaaji gloated, 'I told you! Now ... start writing.'

And I did.

Nothing kept Srilaaji down—not even the pandemic.

Here's sending big, big love to all the wonderful folks at Simon and Schuster India—for 'getting' me and also 'getting' Srilaaji!

She's for real, even if I imagined her.

Shobhaa Dé
Mumbai
17 September 2020